"It's only me."

Nick stepped into the change room and closed the door.

"What are you doing in here?" Liv asked, holding the minuscule lacy bra in front of her.

"This would be a good time to see if you have it in you to be spontaneous," Nick said, reaching for her. The lace didn't conceal her nipples. On the contrary, it created a peekaboo effect that left him a little breathless.

He moved his lips to the hollow of her throat, stroking with his tongue as he kneaded her buttocks.

"Yes, yes," Liv whispered.

He lifted a lace-clad breast in one hand and caressed her hardened nipple with his thumb while he slid the other inside her panties. With more willpower than he knew he possessed, he took his hands away and kissed her softly. They'd spent enough time in the dressing room to make the clerk suspicious.

"The lacy bra will do nicely," he said, winking at the blushing clerk.

Dear Reader,

Who doesn't love the holidays? The lights, the tinsel, the wrapping of gifts, the unwrapping…? Mmm, especially the unwrapping!

When former lovers Liv Kearns and Nick Matheson are reunited, it's strictly business until the layers start coming off! Can public relations professional Liv keep reporter Nick at arm's length?

We (Jennifer Drew is the pseudonym for the mother-daughter writing team of Barbara Andrews and Pam Hanson) hope you enjoy finding out that the answer to this question is a resounding no!

So take a break from the hectic pace of your holiday season and sit back to see what's going to be revealed!

Enjoy!

Jennifer Drew

Books by Jennifer Drew

HARLEQUIN DUETS

*Bad Boy Grooms

JENNIFER DREW

ALL WRAPPED UP

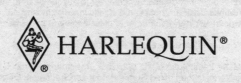

HARLEQUIN®

TORONTO • NEW YORK • LONDON
AMSTERDAM • PARIS • SYDNEY • HAMBURG
STOCKHOLM • ATHENS • TOKYO • MILAN • MADRID
PRAGUE • WARSAW • BUDAPEST • AUCKLAND

This one's for our readers...with heartfelt thanks

ISBN 0-373-69156-4

ALL WRAPPED UP

Copyright © 2003 by Pamela Hanson and Barbara Andrews.

Visit us at www.eHarlequin.com

Printed in U.S.A.

1

LATER SHE'D CRY or scream.

Olivia Kearns pressed her throbbing forehead against the ice-cold, living-room window of her suburban Chicago town house. She wanted to freak out, but now wasn't the time to lose it, not when she had so much to do.

Outside, snow flurries were starting to accumulate. Liv hoped her parents, driving away in separate cars, wouldn't have trouble with the slippery roads. She shook her head in disbelief, still unable to accept that her parents really intended to divorce after nearly thirty years of seemingly harmonious marriage. They'd come to her home to tell her the bad news, calling ahead to be sure she'd be there on a Saturday afternoon. Dad had nodded agreement while her mother assured her the decision was for the best.

Would she and her sister, Amy, have a place they could consider the family home, a place where they could all gather for Christmas? One set of grandparents had retired to Florida and the other set to Arizona, so everyone had always come to her parents' house for family celebrations.

Liv was the family problem-solver, the one who could resolve any crisis—but not this one. How could her parents split up? They were the heart of the family. How could they still be a family if her parents weren't together? Liv knew she was being a drama queen, but she didn't care.

She padded in stocking feet across the moss-green carpeting, hardly seeing her comfy couch and chair covered with flowery slipcovers or the Queen Anne–style cherry tables. The room was tidy and organized, just the way she liked her life.

What she needed to do was make a list. Making a to-do list would help her focus and feel more in control. She went upstairs to her office in the spare bedroom and grabbed a fresh yellow legal pad.

First, she thought, writing a bold numeral one, she had to cancel her parents' New Year's Eve thirtieth-anniversary party.

Theoretically, she and Amy, her older sister by one year, were planning the party, but she'd never expected much help from her sister. Amy was willing enough, but organization wasn't her strong suit especially now when her wedding was coming up in a few months. She had more on her plate than she could manage. It was up to Liv to cancel the party.

She groaned. Nearly fifty invitations had gone out. She'd have to explain fifty times why the party was off.

Then there was Amy's wedding. Only her sister would choose February for a big wedding. Liv had tried to suggest tactfully that sub-zero, snowstormy late winter wasn't the best time. Now it was an awful time because of her parents. Who would keep the wedding arrangements on track? She wrote a large number two on her list.

"I can get through this," she said with a sigh.

She was almost glad there were no men in her life at the moment. She didn't have to break a date to the anniversary party, because her last relationship had ended several months ago. Breaking up with Jerry after a lukewarm relationship had been more comedy than drama, although she wouldn't mind a shoulder to cry on right now.

The timing for a family crisis was terrible. This wasn't a good time to worry about anything but work. She'd done plenty of that lately because the situation there was in constant flux under a new CEO.

William Lawrence Associates was a venerable old public relations firm. She'd worked there since graduating from college five years ago and loved her job specializing in crisis management. It was exciting to work in the heart of Chicago, even though it meant a daily train commute from her town house in Haley Park. She loved being part of a dynamic team and couldn't imagine a job better suited to her talents. Her co-workers were like a second family. Her best friend, Dana Gerard, who had the office next to hers, was like a second sister. The vivacious little brunette could always make Liv smile, even after a grueling day. She felt lucky to have such a positive person in her life.

Liv was a little uneasy about the recent change in leadership. William Lawrence Jr. had just retired, leaving a third-generation Lawrence in control. Billy Lawrence, who refused to be known as William III, wanted to attract hip new clients in the sports and entertainment fields. At twenty-seven Liv was one of their top people, but she'd been advised to update her image and change her attitude. Even though her new boss was close to forty himself, Liv didn't doubt he'd replace her with someone younger if she didn't meet his expectations.

"Loosen up a little," Billy Lawrence had told her.

She wrote "loosen up" on her list and underlined it.

The words were painfully familiar, thanks to her ex-boyfriend, Jerry Lockmor. When he'd dumped her, he'd told her that she was too uptight in bed. Of course, his idea of passion had been thirty-two seconds of foreplay and a neon-colored condom. She'd been hurt when he broke off their relationship, but in retrospect it was a relief to have him out of her life.

"I know what great sex is, Jerry, you idiot," she muttered. "You were never in the ballpark."

She'd always believed in long-lasting relationships because her parents' marriage had flourished. They were forcing her to reconsider her beliefs.

She felt confused and hollow inside, but weeping and wailing wasn't her style. She had things to do.

The phone on the desk right beside her rang. There was no one she was in the mood to talk to at the moment so she let the machine answer it.

"Olivia, pick up the phone. I know you're there. I just talked to Mom."

Her sister was at the top of the list of people she wanted to avoid right now. If anyone could shatter her veneer of self-control, it was Amy.

"Honey, I know you're upset, but I'm going to keep calling until you talk to me. A family needs to pull together at a time like this." Her sister sounded weepy. "We're sisters. We should help each other."

Could things get any worse? How could Liv make Amy feel better when she was miserable herself? Reluctantly she picked up the phone.

"I was in the bathroom," she lied.

"You were right by the phone trying to avoid me. I know it hurts, Liv, having Mom and Dad break up," Amy said. "I cried for days when I learned—"

"You cried for days? When did they tell you?" Liv felt as though she'd been kicked in the stomach.

"They didn't exactly tell me. Well, they did, but only because I knew something was wrong."

"How?" Liv couldn't believe she'd missed something so obvious that her sister had clued in to.

"Mom wasn't into planning my wedding the way she had been. She was distracted," Amy said.

"How long have you known? Why didn't you tell me?"

"I haven't known that long. Mom thought she should tell you herself. Please, don't get upset. It doesn't matter who knew what when. I hate that it's happened, but I'm sure everything will work out. Are you okay?"

That was just great! Amy, who thought a broken fingernail was a major tragedy, was consoling *her*.

"I'll be fine when I get used to the idea of parents who don't love each other anymore. Don't worry about me," Liv said.

"I know, I know, you're the one who always has things under control. But remember, they're still young enough to build new lives."

"I didn't know they hated their old one," Liv said.

Amy rarely played big sister. In fact, Liv sometimes forgot her sibling was one year older. Talking about her parents' bombshell was making it seem all the more real.

"They don't hate each other, they just changed and grew apart," Amy said. "You've probably figured that out for yourself. We have to cancel their anniversary party."

"People don't usually give parties to celebrate a divorce," Liv said, not intentionally sarcastic but it came out that way.

Liv felt numb all over. She didn't want to deal with this. It shouldn't be happening to her family.

"Liv, I feel guilty, but I won't be able to help you call the guests to cancel. It's really hectic at the flower shop. We can hardly keep up with all the orders for Christmas parties. And Sean says he never sees enough of me, so we're going to his parents' in Wisconsin next weekend."

Amy talked rapidly. Now that she'd given her consolation talk, she clearly didn't want to deal with Liv's take on it.

Liv would hate explaining to fifty people why her parents wouldn't be having an anniversary party, but it wasn't as if she had much choice.

"Okay, I'll do it," she said grumpily.

"You're the best! No one ever had a better little sister."

Yeah, yeah. Liv wasn't in the mood for her sister's facile compliments.

"There is one tiny little thing you should know. Do you have pencil and paper handy? Of course you do. You're always so well organized. Write down this number, 555–2996. Got it?"

"Yes, 555–2996. Whose number is it?"

"You didn't have a date for Mom and Dad's party, and I just happened to pick up the sports page of the *Chicago Post*..."

"You never read the sports section." Liv braced herself to hear one more thing she wasn't going to like.

"I was using it to repot a plant. Anyway, there was a story by Nick Matheson, the guy you brought home for Christmas once. He was so cute, and I felt so bad because his parents had just gotten a divorce. I actually envied you—but, of course, Sean suits me perfectly now."

"What are you talking about?"

Even control freaks had a breaking point.

"Nick's back in Chicago working for the *Post*. I sent him an invitation to Mom and Dad's party. That's his number. You'll have to uninvite him."

"Why me?" Liv protested. "You invited him. You should be the one to tell him the party's canceled."

Being dumped by Jerry had stung her ego for about ten seconds, but Nick had really wounded her. She didn't want to dredge up the old heartache by talking to him.

"I don't know him that well. I'm sorry, Liv. I shouldn't have meddled with the guest list."

"You call him!"

"No, really. You should be the one to do it. Oh, I have a call waiting. It's Sean. Love you!"

The phone went dead. Liv realized she was holding her breath.

Nick Matheson.

She'd never completely stopped thinking about him, but she was surprised by the pang of regret she'd felt hearing his name.

Her sister, who floated through life blissfully unaware of subtle nuances in human behavior, had appointed herself matchmaker. Now, typically, she'd dumped the problem on Liv. If she didn't love her sister, she could cheerfully strangle her.

Liv put item number three, call Nick Matheson, on her list. But she wasn't sure she could make herself do it. He might misunderstand and think she was trying to get together with him again. How humiliating would that be?

Once she'd really wanted the kind of relationship her parents had, but she'd made the bad mistake of falling in love with Nick who had no intention of making a long-term commitment. She couldn't believe Amy had stuck her with the job of telling him the party was off. It had been five years since he'd left her, and she dreaded having to speak to him.

They'd met when she was a senior at Northwestern. He'd been a graduate student in journalism, and they'd met in a seminar she'd gotten special permission to take. The first time he walked into the room, she'd wanted him. He was tall, lean and good-looking, with sandy-blond hair and deep blue eyes that made her tingle whenever he looked at her. But he was a lot more than a handsome face. His sharp wit and warmth had overwhelmed her.

Now Nick was ancient history, but they had one new thing in common.

Ironically, it was his parents' divorce that had brought them together. He'd needed sympathy and understanding, and she'd been more than willing to give it.

She'd needed to believe that he'd loved her, at least a little, even though he'd repeatedly warned her from the beginning he wasn't into commitment. At first she'd blamed his attitude on the shock of his parents' breakup.

She'd been so naive, thinking she could change his mind over time. Well, she'd been dead wrong, and had paid a big price in heartache for dreaming she could make Nick into something he wasn't. Pushing hard for commitment, she'd ended up with him moving on and out of her life.

The last thing she wanted was for him to think she was mooning over him.

At least having a lot to do would help her cope with her parents' divorce. Doing things efficiently was second nature, probably a genetic gift from her father who ran his insurance business like a military operation. Amy took after Mom, who could charm people into buying real estate but struggled with the details of finalizing a sale.

Liv went to her kitchen with its pale yellow cupboards and uncluttered green marbleized countertops. While she boiled water for tea, she vowed not to feel sorry for herself. The divorce wasn't about her. The important thing was whether her parents would be happier apart, but she was having trouble believing they would be. They'd always seemed so right together, so close they could complete each other's sentences.

She carried the mug of tea back to her office to begin making calls. She couldn't spare a minute at work for personal business. Her job was difficult enough without trying to impress a new boss with how hip, with-it and on top of things she was, his latest additions to her job description. She found the party list and punched in the first number on her phone.

A few minutes later she'd talked to one person and left three messages on answering machines. She was calling Nick next. It was ridiculous to stew over talking to a man she hadn't seen in five years. The sooner she did it, the quicker she could forget him again.

Liv still vividly remembered her anger and hurt when she'd caught him at a party with a frizzy-haired blonde on his lap. He'd ditched the girl and taken Liv home to the little apartment she shared with two friends, but it had been the beginning of the end. They never slept together again, never spent long hours in companionable silence in the library, never took long walks or drove in his car to watch Lake Michigan lapping at the shoreline of Chicago.

He'd left a void in her life and in her heart. Maybe that was why no man since had measured up to her expectations.

She punched in Nick's number. What if he thought the invitation had been her idea? Would he think she was chasing him? Did he think she'd hop into bed with him for old time's sake, as if he was so irresistible she still got hot and bothered just thinking about him? The possibilities made her cringe. How could Amy have put her in this position?

His phone rang three times. She took a deep breath and hoped her nerve wouldn't fail her. He most likely hadn't given her a thought in years before Amy called him. Liv didn't know where he'd been or what he'd been doing for five years, but she'd bet he hadn't been lonely for female companionship. He attracted women like no man she'd ever dated, maybe because he genuinely liked to spend time with them. He had a gift for listening and making people feel better about themselves.

"This is Nick Matheson. I'm not available now but leave your name and number. I'll get back to you as soon as I can."

His answering machine. What a relief, even though hearing his recorded message made her quiver. He had a deep, mellow voice that matched his drop-dead good looks. She could see him in her mind, tall at six-two with blond hair and bedroom-blue eyes lively with intelligence and passion.

The machine beeped, and she had to leave a message. Now that she'd heard his voice, she'd never work up enough nerve to call back.

"This is Olivia Kearns. Don't bother coming to my parents' party."

She'd meant to explain that Amy had sent the invitation and the party had been canceled.

"Don't bother coming," she repeated, not at all pleased with herself. She'd gotten rattled and left a terribly abrupt message.

Should she call back and leave another, more tactful message? What if he answered himself on the second try? What if he...? He loved afternoon sex—he'd been pretty fond of it anytime, but stealing a little time out of a busy day had once been great for both of them. It would be terrible to interrupt something like that. He might be living with someone, and she might cause trouble for him by calling twice.

Face it, she was afraid of how she'd react if she had to talk to him. She didn't want to awaken feelings she'd long ago buried. No, a second call was a very bad idea.

She slashed his name off her list with a black felt pen.

NICK HAD GOTTEN HOME from his wasted weekend too late Sunday night to bother checking his messages. He couldn't believe he'd hung around the little lakeside town of Saint Joseph, Michigan, for two days without getting an interview with the daughter of a depression-era baseball player.

It didn't deter him that a couple of other *Post* reporters had tried and failed in the past few weeks. In fact, he loved the challenge of succeeding where his more seasoned colleagues had struck out. He was the new kid in the sports department, and he wanted to cement his reputation by interviewing the reclusive Matilda Merris, daughter of the baseball player who'd rocked Chicago with a bribery scandal in the 1930s. There were lots of questions only she could answer. Had the infamous Marty Merris been intimidated by gangsters? Were some leading politicians of the day involved? What had been her father's motivation in accepting money to throw a crucial game?

He didn't usually write history, but Merris was a special case. Marty was one of the greatest athletes that sport had ever seen, single-handedly exciting interest in a new league that failed not long after his disgrace. Sports-crazy Chicago was opening a new sports museum soon, and the directors were determined to keep Merris out of it. Mack Gallagher, Nick's editor at the *Post*, had a collection of Merris memorabilia he wanted to donate to the new museum, but so far the powers that be had refused it.

They wanted to write Chicago's third great team out of the history books.

Nick had already figured out that the *Post* had more reporters than they needed to keep up with local sports. If the big bosses ever came to the same conclusion, he wanted to be too invaluable to be let go. Getting the Merris story could be his ticket to fame—and job security, no small prize in a field as competitive as his.

If he could uncover the true story of Chicago's biggest sports scandal, there was a more immediate payoff. Mack had promised him better assignments if he could justify what Merris had done.

Nick had a file two inches thick, much of it gathered by the two reporters who'd given up on the piece. Without the insights only Matilda Merris could provide, the story was only speculation. The fact that two of his co-workers had failed only challenged him.

He started listening to his messages, first one from his mother in Florida. She wanted him to spend Christmas with her. He wanted to see her but no way could he leave Chicago now. Nor was he keen to hang out with her second husband, Terry, who called him "son" and treated him like a ten-year-old. Maybe he'd drive to Springfield for the holiday. He hadn't seen Dad and his second wife in quite a while. Or maybe not. Things were getting interesting in the Windy City.

"Don't bother coming to the party."

He'd been absentmindedly checking other messages, but this one caught his full attention. He replayed it. Yeah, he'd heard right. It was Liv Kearns telling him not to "bother" coming to a party.

After five years she couldn't even say, "Hi, Nick," before she canceled the invitation to her parents' anniversary party?

He played the message a third time. Couldn't she at least say *please* don't come? If she didn't want him there, why had he gotten an invitation? He hadn't decided whether to go, but, truth to tell, he hadn't been back in the area long enough to have much of a social life. He'd been tempted to go until he remembered the last time they'd been together. He'd tried to explain why he wasn't ready for commitment. She knew how much he was keyed up to begin his career, and she knew, too, that his father's failure in marriage made Nick question his own chance of success.

If there was anything in his life he regretted, it was his breakup with Liv. He'd been more in love with her than any woman before or after. He'd been a jerk—with good reason. Even before his parents' divorce, he hadn't been a fan of commitment. Still wasn't, considering that he'd left his job in Kansas City when sexy Darla, a career-driven lawyer, had started dropping wedding hints.

He loved sports and loved writing about them. It was a lifestyle that didn't leave room for domestic entanglements or exclusive dating. Liv had tempted him once. All the more reason why he should've turned down the party invitation when he first got it. Maybe part of him wanted to see her again, but he was relieved that she'd made the decision for him.

Liv might have made him change his mind if he'd allowed their relationship to continue. He still got turned on by hearing her voice, but he'd been too ambitious—and face it, too immature—to consider a serious commitment five years ago. He'd never deceived her about that, but he shouldn't have started something he couldn't finish. In the beginning he hadn't expected to care for her as much as he had. The longer he'd been with her, the more she expected their relationship to be permanent. He'd done her a favor by ending it, but he knew she hadn't seen it that way.

He played her message a fourth time. He wasn't imagining the breathy, seductive tone of her voice, even though her words were cold. That was typical of Liv. On the surface she was an ice princess, but he'd experienced the passion that simmered under the surface. She'd been hot, all he could want in bed and more.

She was totally genuine and natural. That was part of what had made their short relationship sizzle. But she didn't have a clue how sexy she was. He'd had to work to unlock her passion, but it had been worth it. She'd rocked his world. He knew pretty much what he wanted in a woman, and he couldn't help wondering what Liv was like now.

Back when they were together, Liv had been sure he'd change his mind about a permanent relationship. Her cure for his commitment phobia had been an excessive dose of devotion on her part. He wasn't proud of it, but she'd scared him off.

He lived for the present. It wasn't like him to second-guess decisions or brood over past mistakes. If Liv was uncomfortable having him come to her parents' party, it was fine with him. His attitude toward relationships had remained the same since they'd parted company. He worked long hours and covered a lot of night and weekend events. He didn't have time for anything but casual relationships, not if he wanted to excel in his field. And he did want that.

He had to get to work. After wasting a whole weekend trying to nail down an interview with Matilda Merris, even standing outside her house in the cold and looking pathetic in the hope she'd give in, he did have one more lead to follow. The old woman was a minor talent in the art world. She was on the client list of a Chicago public relations firm, William Lawrence Associates. Maybe, if he got really lucky, someone there would use their clout to get him inside Matilda's Michigan home.

He dressed in gray flannel slacks, gray turtleneck, a navy blazer and tasseled loafers to impress the people at the PR firm. The gang in the newsroom would razz him about his dated preppy look, but he was at the end of his rope with this story. A whole lot of background work would go to waste if he couldn't persuade the fallen hero's daughter to talk to him.

Later, when he had time, he might give Liv a lesson in phone etiquette. He wondered if she still wore that flowery perfume that had turned him on, but it looked as if he'd never get close enough to know.

Mostly he wondered if she still hated him.

2

"I LOVE THIS LIFE," Liv muttered to herself as she hung her midcalf black coat on the hall tree in the corner of her cubicle.

Mostly it was true. She didn't mind riding the Metra System from Roselle, the stop closest to her home in Haley Park, to Union Station. She usually enjoyed the three-block walk from the terminal to the tall gray building where William Lawrence Associates occupied a suite on the ninth floor. She didn't even mind the small, crowded cubicle that served as her office, although neon lights were no substitute for a window.

Once she got immersed in the business of the day, she rarely noticed the blandness of her surroundings. Her office was one of four created when a storage room had been divided into cubicles.

Today was Monday, always a busy day, but it wasn't starting at all well. For one thing, her college intern was there ahead of her working at one of the two computers in the room. Liv didn't exactly dislike Brandi Jo Willis, but sharing the small space with her was like having sand stuck in her swimsuit.

This morning the too-perky twenty-one-year-old blonde was dressed for success in a black jersey suit with a skirt that barely managed to cover her panties. The jacket was short, buttoned to hug her waist, and had a plunging neckline. She was obviously wearing nothing under it.

"Good morning, Miss Kearns," Brandi Jo said, refusing to call Liv by her first name, a mockery of respect that annoyed Liv. "Mr. Bosworth asked me to finish some work for him. You don't mind, do you?"

"No, that's fine," Liv lied. "How long will it take? I planned on having you do some research for me."

In fact, she really needed help today. She felt mentally and emotionally drained after canceling her parents' party. Even the people she'd notified by e-mail had called her for details about the divorce.

Liv pulled her white wrap sweater more tightly around her, still shivering from the walk through bone-chilling blasts of wind. The second week in December was beginning, and arctic winds were bombarding the Windy City. Unlike Brandi Jo, she'd dressed for the weather in black trousers and a turtleneck under her sweater, but she still couldn't seem to warm up.

"Boz, I mean Mr. Bosworth, said to take as long as I need to do this," Brandi Jo said.

"Of course he did," Liv said under her breath.

Ray Bosworth, Boz to his friends, was the vice president in charge of media and her immediate superior.

"He wants me to work here when my internship is over," Brandi Jo said without looking up from the computer screen.

No surprise there, Liv thought. Boz was infamous for chasing interns. Opinion was divided on whether he ever caught any.

"That reminds me. I have to do your evaluation for school. When is it due?" Liv asked.

"Anytime before January tenth." The intern sounded a little less sure of herself. She still had to graduate.

Liv planned to give her a good report card, so to speak, because it would be petty and spiteful not to acknowledge that the girl did work hard. But Liv didn't have any illusions about her temporary helper. The intern was auditioning for a job with William Lawrence Associates, and that job could very well be Liv's.

Was it a sign of her shrinking status that others didn't bother to knock on the closed door of her office? With Brandi Jo entrenched in her space, the yellowish room with dark olive carpeting felt even less like a private work area.

Boz, as Liv called him in her mind but never aloud, barged in and sat down in Liv's chair before she had a chance to get started on anything.

"Good morning, Ray," she said, put in the position of standing at attention in front of him.

"I knew you'd want to hear about Friday's executive meeting," he said self-importantly.

Most days Liv liked Boz well enough, even though he could be pompous. The round, graying VP was a professional glad-hander, and, to his credit, he was usually as pleasant to employees as to clients.

"I haven't had a chance to call up the minutes," Liv admitted.

"There's going to be a slight shift in your duties, Liv. Nothing major right away, but we'll be easing you into new responsibilities," Bosworth said, suddenly intent on examining his fingernails.

"What kind of shift?" Out of the corner of her eye she saw Brandi had stopped working to listen.

"Billy wants more emphasis on client relations. You'll be expected to generate new leads and work up some accounts of your own. Gradually we'll take you out of crisis management in favor of having your own client base."

"But crisis management is my specialty," she protested.

"And you're good at it." Boz tried to smile benevolently, but he was looking at Brandi, not Liv. "This is your opportunity to grow with the firm, be on the cutting edge of expansion."

She got it. She had to generate new business.

"The firm will supply you with leads, but you'll do your old job until you have developed a new client base." He stood and smoothed his dark charcoal jacket, as though it could conceal his barrel belly. "Remember, Liv, Billy wants you to loosen up. Dress more youthfully. Maybe Brandi Jo could give you a few pointers."

Or maybe, Liv thought angrily, I should cruise the South Side and see what the girls on the street are wearing.

"You know, Billy takes a personal interest in every employee," Boz said sanctimoniously. "He's our team leader. He wants success for his employees as much as for himself, and we need a whole new slate of hip clients."

"I love helping clients who have real problems," Liv said. "I love the challenge of putting out fires."

"Well, it wouldn't hurt you to start a few," her boss said dryly, dropping his good-guy act. "Brandi Jo, can I see you in my office?"

Liv watched the intern totter out on three-inch heels. How could Boz dump on her in front of an intern? Maybe he'd done it to encourage Brandi Jo. Maybe Liv's job would be available sooner than she thought.

Liv tried to convince herself that change was sometimes good, but she didn't like Boz's explanation. It sounded like a sink-or-swim situation, not an opportunity for advancement.

She had no choice but to try to meet her boss's expectations, but she would not consult Brandi Jo Willis for tips on how to dress. What did her bosses want, tight low-rise pants and a pierced navel?

Unfortunately, Billy wanted her to look sexy in hopes of enticing new clients for the agency. She wasn't high enough up the ladder to get a chance at major accounts, so her life would degenerate into a series of tedious lunches and meetings with restaurant owners, club managers and other small-time hotshots.

Meanwhile, what did she have to do to appease the new president of the firm? Darned if she'd copy Brandi's style, but there were some things she could do.

First, the black turtleneck had to go. Her office was warm enough to wear her sweater without it. The white cashmere plunged to a deep V but tied securely at her waist. She'd spend her day trying to keep it together so her bra wouldn't show, but at least it would demonstrate she was trying to loosen up.

She'd dawdled too long to waste more time going to the inconveniently located women's restroom at the end of the outer corridor. It would only take a few seconds to peel off the turtleneck and slip back into her sweater. She stood and quickly started stripping, not really wanting to get caught in the act by her snotty little intern.

The air was cool on her bare shoulders and back, and she shivered in her lacy peach bra.

When a sharp knock on the door startled her, she called emphatically, "Wait just a minute."

The dark oak door banged inward on loose hinges, and she faced her visitor in an underwire bra that gave her enough uplift to launch a rocket.

"Now, that's what I call effective public relations," the newcomer said, pushing the door shut without taking his eyes off her cleavage.

"Nick!"

"Do you do a striptease for all your potential clients?" He had a devilish smile, and he beamed it at her full force.

She was too stunned to continue dressing. Five years had weathered the last vestiges of boyishness from Nick Matheson's face, but his deep-set eyes were as blue and penetrating as ever.

"What are you doing here?"

"Sorry. The receptionist said to walk right in." He turned his back to her.

"Are you a potential client?"

Her fingers felt thick and clumsy, but she managed to get into the sweater and yank the ties into a tight knot.

"Not exactly."

"It's been a long time," she said. "How have you been?" Other than gorgeous, sexy and cocky.

"Fine."

"You can turn around now. How did you know I work here?"

She tried not to squirm as he turned and gazed at her.

"You still look spectacular, Liv."

"Thanks."

He still had the annoying habit of dodging questions, but her own reaction concerned her more. How could he possibly look even better at twenty-nine than he had as a twenty-four-year-old graduate student? He was dressed in a conservative jacket and slacks, a big step up from the jeans and sweatshirts he used to live in, but his long, lanky body looked even harder and more muscular. His hair was shorter but still combed back from his forehead. He was clean-shaven, and his skin had a honey glow with high color in his cheeks from the cold outside.

"If you came for an apology, I'm sorry."

"Oh, your message." His little grin vanished. "My dentist leaves a friendlier one."

"I'm sorry about that. I was upset."

"Because your sister invited me? If you didn't want me to be there, it's okay."

She was touched that Nick cared enough to look her up, but rattled because her heart was pounding. She had to fight a crazy urge to jump into his arms and kiss him silly.

She'd imagined seeing him by accident someday, maybe on the street or at a party. She'd thought up all kinds of clever, witty comments to show him that she was over him, so why couldn't she remember a single one now?

"It's not that. The party is canceled. My parents won't be celebrating their thirtieth anniversary because they're getting a divorce."

"Liv, I'm really sorry. I know what a blow it is when parents split."

"Yeah, and I never saw it coming."

"If it's any consolation, mine are much happier apart. They've both remarried and like their new lives."

"Well, I'm sorry my message was so abrupt. I'd just found out, and I had so many people to call and—" She started twisting the ties of her sweater then forced herself to stop. She'd been calm and collected talking to her parents' friends and canceling the party. It was what everyone expected of her, and more importantly what she demanded of herself. She took a deep breath, then another, locking her arms across her chest. Nick meant nothing to her anymore, so why was she feeling so emotional?

"No problem," he interrupted. "You didn't even know your sister had invited me, did you?"

"Well, actually no."

Now that the initial shock of seeing him was wearing off, she remembered the months of heartbreak after he'd left her. She wasn't a girl to put her hand on a hot burner twice.

"Well, thank you for coming by."

"Actually, seeing you is only a bonus. I didn't know you worked here. I'm chasing a lead on a story."

Nick *always* had an ulterior motive—the warm glow she was feeling at seeing him again was replaced by icy suspicion.

"Here?" she asked.

"Your firm represents someone I badly need to interview."

"We don't divulge client information."

"Yes, I've already been told that, but the receptionist hinted you might be able to help me."

Mary, the receptionist, was fifty-seven and seven times a grandmother. Was there no female who was immune to Nick's charms? At least Liv knew *she* was.

"She was mistaken," Liv said.

"If I could explain—"

"I'm sorry, Nick, but William Lawrence Associates keeps all client information confidential."

"Let me tell you what I'm after, then I'll accept your decision, whatever it is," he said.

He was relentless. Soon she was going to be wrapping her sweater ties around his gorgeous neck. "You aren't going to talk me into betraying a client," she said.

"I don't even know if you still represent this one. Let me take you to lunch," he urged. "We can talk about it."

"Thank you, no. I don't have time to go out for lunch."

"Then let me take you to dinner, unless you have to hurry home to someone," he said.

"No, I live alone, but dinner isn't a good idea."

"We'll go someplace close and quick." Another thing hadn't changed. He didn't like to take no for an answer.

Liv noticed Brandi Jo standing in the doorway watching with wide eyes. Did she think Liv was so old she was on the shelf?

"All right," Liv said impulsively. "Meet me down in the lobby at five-thirty."

"I didn't know you had company," Brandi Jo said, moving over to her computer table and openly checking out Nick.

Brandi Jo's buttocks had a life of their own under the clingy skirt, and Nick couldn't help but notice her backfield-in-motion bid for his attention.

"This is Nick Matheson, sportswriter for the *Post*," Liv said dryly. "He's just leaving."

"I'm Brandi Jo Willis, Miss Kearns's intern." She directed a high-wattage smile Nick's way.

"Nice to meet you," he said, to his credit not rising to Brandi Jo's bait. "I'll see you at five-thirty, Liv."

He backed toward the door and left without giving Brandi Jo the appraising look she usually received from men.

Liv realized that she'd let all her stored-up annoyance with the intern trap her into meeting Nick for dinner. For a moment she'd enjoyed showing the little sexpot that she could attract men too, but it was a short-lived triumph. It was a really bad idea to see Nick again for any reason. She was totally over him and wanted to stay that way.

3

STANDING IN the lobby of the Syracuse Building where she worked, Liv stared at a tiny butterfly in the design on one of the elevator doors, a detail she hadn't noticed in the five years she'd worked there. Of course, she'd never stood in the lobby for nearly twenty minutes. Dana and several other people stopped to ask if Liv needed anything as she waited and waited for Nick to arrive. Time meant nothing to Nick, one more reason why she was fortunate their relationship had ended.

Even the two uniformed security guards sitting in the cubicle where they monitored cameras were beginning to look at her too frequently for comfort. She knew the routine, of course. At six sharp the door would be locked. Then no one, not even fast-talking Nick Matheson, could get in without buzzing and showing a special identity card.

She'd had it with waiting. She turned up her coat collar and braced herself to fight Chicago wind and commuter crowds. If the snow kept falling in big fluffy clumps, the lot where she'd left her car would be snowed shut before she got there for the last lap of her trip home. She hoped her temperamental little compact, seven years old and counting, would start.

Nick stepped out of the snowy darkness just as she opened the door. She met him on the pavement where wet slushy snow was already as high as the ankles of her boots.

"Thanks for waiting," he said with a lopsided grin. "I got held up."

He was wearing a red squall jacket, the hood hanging down and filling with snow. Nick never covered his head in less than a raging blizzard, Liv remembered. She had to resist an urge to brush silvery flakes from his hair.

"I only wanted to tell you I can't have dinner," she said. "The way it's snowing, I'll be lucky to get home before the streets drift shut."

"You drive into the city? Where do you live?" he asked, stomping snow from his boots.

"Haley Park. I take the train, but I have to drive home from the station."

"Have dinner with me, and I'll drive you home. You can take a cab to your car in the morning."

"No thanks to both. I'm going to take the Metra."

"It's no trouble. I've got four-wheel drive, and I pretty much go in your direction anyway. I live in Ira Heights."

Nick took her arm as the door behind them opened. A couple came out, and she got a glimpse of the man, tall and broad-shouldered with a big square face, a felt derby and a tan wool overcoat. She opened her mouth to acknowledge the president of William Lawrence Associates, but Billy wasn't looking in her direction. He was too busy gazing fondly down on Brandi Jo's sleek blond head.

She should've known.

Liv scooted around Nick and started to walk away before Brandi Jo saw her, not that the intern wasn't fully focused on her conquest. Liv feared her job was toast. The intern had one more semester before graduation, then Billy might slot her into Liv's position.

The restructuring was a ruse as far as she was concerned. They were setting her up to fail. If she couldn't attract the kind of new clients Billy wanted, he'd use it as an excuse to replace her with Brandi Jo. The whole staff would shake their heads and say, "Poor Liv couldn't hack it."

"Where are you going?" Nick asked. He was half running and half sliding to keep up with her on the slushy sidewalk.

"You wanted dinner. Let's have dinner," she said, too upset about Brandi Jo to worry about catching a train.

"I had in mind a little Italian place," he said. "We're going in the wrong direction."

She wanted to explode. Had he conveniently forgotten how they'd loved romantic Italian dinners? It was the worst possible restaurant choice after what he'd done to her five years ago. She stopped and took a deep breath.

Her parents were splitting up. Her job was in jeopardy. Now Nick had barged back into her life and wanted her to do something that could violate client confidentiality. She might as well pig out on pasta and get fat.

"Fine," she said sharply. "Where is it?"

She'd retreated far enough so there was no danger of catching up with Billy and Brandi Jo. Dinner with Nick was just what she needed to cap off a perfectly awful day.

NICK OFFERED LIV his arm, but she stubbornly refused it even though the sidewalk was as slippery as a toboggan run. The way she was stomping along, she was cruising for a fall. She was so hostile he had second thoughts about dinner.

"Hey, slow down," he said. "No rush to get to the restaurant. The Milano won't be crowded on a night like this."

Maybe he was crazy to take her to a cozy little

place. The last thing he wanted was to start something with her. She took life much too seriously for him. Breaking up with her once had been hard enough. He still had residual guilt and absolutely did not want to go through that again. Maybe if she hadn't been standing there in her office in a lacy bra...

Sometimes a good memory was a pain. He could recall every important play in a game and write a story about it with minimal notes, but he could also remember the rosy-brown pebbling around Liv's nipples and the way they used to harden under his tongue. The downy auburn hair on her mound was the softest thing he'd ever touched, and he hoped she hadn't started shaving it as his last girlfriend had. Bristles were a turnoff, not that he would ever have sex with Liv again.

"How far is this place?" Liv asked, still sounding angry.

"Another block."

They were waiting for a stoplight along with a few other people with heads bowed against the blinding snow.

Nick needed to concentrate on the favor he wanted from Liv. She wouldn't be easy to convince, but instead of planning a good argument, he was remembering her dewy-eyed look after sex. He even remembered the cute little mole on her butt and the bright red polish she'd worn on her toes when they'd celebrated Christmas Eve in the middle of the night under her parents' Christmas tree. The next day she'd blushed every time he hinted at it, but he'd never unwrapped a package as exciting as Liv.

She barged past the steps leading down to the Milano. He caught her arm to stop her.

"Here's the restaurant," he said.

"Ah, basement cuisine. Charming."

"You didn't used to be sarcastic." He took her elbow because snow had drifted onto the concrete steps, and he didn't want her to slip.

"I used to be—" She broke off whatever she'd intended to say.

He opened the door and let her go ahead of him. Hopefully they could get through the meal without a trip down memory lane. He wasn't proud of the way he'd broken off their relationship, but it wouldn't do his cause any good to rehash it.

The restaurant wasn't crowded. Less than half of the round tables with green-and-white-checkered tablecloths were occupied. Nick spotted an empty one against the far wall.

"Okay if we sit over there, Tony?" he asked the lean, hawk-nosed waiter with a white apron tied tightly around his waist.

"Sure thing, Nick."

He guided Liv over to the table, leery of putting his hand on her arm again. Tonight he had to concentrate on getting her help. When he took her coat, he noticed Liv was wearing a black turtleneck like armor under her sweater.

"He knows you by name?" she asked. "Have you been working in Chicago long enough to be chummy with waiters?"

"I've been at the *Post* since September. Once people find out I'm a sportswriter, they like talking to me. Everyone in Chicago thinks and lives sports."

"I don't," she said dryly.

"You used to love baseball," he reminded her.

"I've grown up. I don't have time for games."

He was pretty sure she was playing one now, but he didn't know what the rules were yet. She knew he wanted something from her. If she hated him so much, why was she here? He was a little nervous about it, which was pretty unusual for him.

Tony came over to the table with spicy Italian sausages standing on end in a basket, a tradition at the Milano, and a small loaf of hard-crusted bread on a wooden board.

"What can I get you and the pretty lady to drink, Nick?"

"A bottle of Chianti, unless you'd like something else?" he asked Liv.

"Whatever you want," she said indifferently.

She seemed determined not to enjoy having dinner with him, but Nick liked a challenge. Liv was going to have a good time if he had to do handstands on the table to amuse her. He realized he wanted to please her, and it had nothing to do with his job.

He sliced the bread and pushed it toward her, then picked up a sausage and chewed it with relish.

"These are delicious. Try one."

She hesitated. Given her mood, he expected a lecture on eating fatty food, but instead she chose one of the meat sticks and delicately nibbled at it.

"It is good." She sounded surprised.

He watched her lips pucker around the finger-shaped sausage. If she was trying to torment him, she'd succeeded. She looked sexier munching the sausage than she had in a skimpy bra, and he was getting hard against his will. He adjusted the tablecloth to make sure it was covering his lap.

"Try the bread," he suggested.

He wasn't sure how he could persuade her to help him, but he had to stay focused. Liv was pretty much his last chance.

Tony came with the wine, popping the cork before

he set it on the table. He poured an inch of the red liquid into a goblet and handed it to Nick.

Nick was no connoisseur, but he knew the taste test was part of the ritual. He sipped and pronounced the wine satisfactory, then watched as the waiter poured for Liv.

"Cheers," Nick said, raising his glass.

"Could we see a menu, please?" Liv asked, half-heartedly raising her glass to his.

"There aren't any menus," Nick quickly said. "Tony will tell us what's good today."

"You got a game to cover tonight?" the waiter asked, not concealing his disappointment at their unseemly haste.

Nick knew a good Italian dinner was supposed to be an event that took hours. The Milano was a great place to bring a date when he was trying to get lucky. A couple of bottles of wine and some groping under the table, and anything could happen.

That wasn't why he was here with Liv. She was still the kind of woman who wanted to settle down—not that he didn't plan to himself sometime in the future, but definitely not now. First he wanted to make a reputation and get a shot at a local column, then maybe syndication or a chance to be an editor. He wasn't as driven as some reporters, but he was ambitious.

"My friend has to catch a train," Nick explained.

"Yeah, I guess the weather is going to get worse," Tony said. "Lousy climate for human beings. If the Cubs ever leave town, I'm outta here."

"So what do you recommend?" Nick asked, trying not to watch as Liv devoured another sausage with puckered lips and licked away the grease with the tip of her tongue. Lips like hers were wasted on a stick of meat.

"Prawns in garlic butter and linguini with clam sauce."

Tony was telling them what to have, not offering choices, but he never steered Nick wrong.

"Sounds great," Nick agreed. "Is that all right with you, Liv?"

He knew she loved prawns, and linguini with clam sauce was one of her favorites. He was surprised when she rejected the waiter's suggestions.

"I'd like a plate of spaghetti with meat sauce and garlic bread. Lots of garlic bread."

She smiled sweetly at the waiter and gave Nick a defiant look. He had a bad feeling. She wasn't going to be convinced of anything tonight. Worse, he was more interested in talking with her than in convincing her to help him. He remembered how much he used to enjoy her lively conversation and humorous take on things.

By the time he'd refilled her wineglass three times to his one, Nick was pretty sure he was going to strike out on enlisting Liv's help. Among other things, his timing was bad. She wasn't taking her parents' divorce at all well.

"Are your parents really happy now?" she asked after they'd pretty much covered their careers for the last five years including her worries about losing her job.

"I think so," he said, glad he could give her some reassurance. "Mom seems to like her new husband. Dad's wife is forty trying to look twenty, but they enjoy going to flea markets and auctions together."

Tony brought their meals in record time. Nick loaded up on prawns and pasta because the waiter, who was also part owner, took it personally if customers didn't stuff themselves. Liv inhaled the spaghetti and drank more wine with uncharacteristic gusto.

"I'm really good at what I do," she said. "I should be vice president instead of that prick Boz."

Nick suspected she was drunk. The prim-and-proper Liv that he knew thought a prick was something you got from a thorn.

Would he be evil if he took advantage of her unhappiness at work to get what he wanted? His editor would say, "Get the story regardless of what you have to do." But this was Liv, and he wasn't sure how far he should go.

"I'm supposed to loosen up, be more spontaneous.... Kind of like you," she said after a moment's hesitation.

"Is that why you were doing a striptease in your office?"

"He wanted me to ask my intern for hints on how to dress!" She put down her fork and bristled with indignation. "That blond babe is after my job!"

Nick laughed. He couldn't help it.

"It's not funny, Nick! I love my job. I don't want to look for a new one."

"I can't imagine anyone being dumb enough to fire you," he said, meaning it. "You're smart, clever and—"

"Dull, conservative—"

"Never dull," he interrupted. "I was never bored with you."

"I wish I knew how to be like you...reckless, daring, spontaneous. Remember when you talked me into driving to Milwaukee in the middle of the night? We both had tons of work for school, but we drove halfway there for no reason at all and ended up in a bar in some little town in Wisconsin."

He remembered all right. When they got back, they'd had fantastic sex in his apartment. He'd never forget the rocking chair or the way she'd thrown aside all her inhibitions for a change.

"It was fun. You were fun."

"You made me have fun. You always had all the good ideas."

He didn't want to play the remember-when game with a woman he'd once been crazy about. But whatever else Liv was, she wasn't spontaneous. She couldn't stand to be out of control in any situation. He'd literally bolted for his life when she started mentioning marriage. In her mind it had been the next logical step in their relationship, but it wasn't for him. He didn't understand why they couldn't just enjoy things the way they were.

"I wish you could tell me how to be spontaneous," she said.

She sounded deeply unhappy, and he was sure the wine had nothing to do with it.

"I don't think it's something you can learn."

"You could show me how to loosen up." She sounded surprised by her own idea. "We can make a deal. Just a little help with a work problem."

He shrugged dismissively, not at all liking the way this reunion with Liv was going. Did she mean what she was saying?

He could think of lots of ways she could loosen up—all of them fun for him. He'd start by burning all her cotton panties. Come to think of it, she'd look spectacular in a black thong. And she'd have to get rid of her sex-only-in-bed mentality. He wondered if Tony had a storeroom they could use. Or he could ride home on the train with her.

But he was pretty damn sure his fantasies had nothing to do with the loosening up she had in mind.

"I'm good at work problems. That's what I do, crisis management at William Lawrence Associates. But I'm afraid I won't be able to change the way they want me to, and Brandi Jo will get my job."

"Brandi Jo?"

"My intern," she said, sounding more like the cranky woman he'd brought to the restaurant. "You met her in my office. If you can show me how to loosen up and be spontaneous, I'll do whatever I can for you."

"I'll walk you to Union Station, and we'll talk about it," Nick said, signaling Tony for the bill.

"We'll help each other," she said emphatically.

"You may want to think about it a little more first," he warned.

"No, I make good snap decisions."

He fervently hoped Liv would be stone cold sober by the time they got to the station so they could talk rationally. As for wanting to sleep with her, what man wouldn't?

His memory was too vivid for comfort. He remembered all the things about her that turned him on, especially the way she liked to tease his ear with her tongue and run her nails over his skin. Maybe because she'd been so cool and restrained at first, it had been doubly exciting when she lost her initial inhibitions. He could remember the first time she'd tasted him with her tongue as clearly as if it had been yesterday. He'd given up a lot when he left Liv. Part of him still regretted it.

He took a deep breath and stood up. He had a story to get, but no way would he get involved with Liv again. She was beautiful, clever and amusing, but she was a woman who wanted commitment.

To do his job, he had to be available whenever there was a sporting event to cover. That meant lots of night work and few free weekends. He hadn't met any woman who would put up with his hours, and he didn't want a life punctuated by arguments and guilt trips. More importantly, he didn't want to be responsible for another person's happiness. A good relationship demanded a whole lot of compromise. His father had never been able to do it, much to his mother's sorrow. He didn't have any reason to believe he'd be better at it.

Liv was more mature now. She was hurting from her parents' breakup and worried about her job, but she certainly hadn't leaped at the chance to go to dinner with him. He didn't deserve a second chance with Liv, and it was far safer for him if he didn't get one.

4

LIV WAS SHIVERING. She'd started as soon as they left the overheated little restaurant and now, within sight of Union Station, she had to clench her jaw shut so Nick wouldn't hear her teeth chattering.

Now that the pleasant glow from the wine had dissipated, she was on edge. She knew better than to get involved with Nick in any way whatsoever. She was older and wiser than she'd been five years ago, but her heart wasn't armor plated. When he smiled, she could feel her resistance melting. Liv was afraid he could persuade her to rob a bank if he turned on his charm full force.

"I'll wait until your train comes," he offered, following her into the cavernous interior of the station.

"You don't need to. It will be nearly half an hour."

"We still have to talk about our deal," he reminded her. "Do you want to sit?"

"No, it feels good to walk after all that food."

If they sat, she'd have to look at Nick. She'd see the way his eyebrows arched and his blue eyes gleamed when he was making a point. The erotic fullness of his lower lip and the hard, masculine line of his jaw might sway her. She'd seen quite enough of Nick Matheson's handsome face and devilish grin for one evening.

She'd recklessly offered to help him if he helped her. She was already regretting it.

The station was pretty full for a snowy evening, and the massive high-roofed terminal dwarfed those who were waiting for trains. It felt odd to be with Nick. They passed the crowded Amtrak waiting area, and began a second circuit of the building.

"Have you changed your mind about our helping each other?" she asked. "It would be strictly a business arrangement."

"Keeping our relationship professional is good. I was thinking about what you want *me* to do. How can I help you loosen up? You were never inclined to go along with my suggestions."

"What about the time we rented three old horror movies?" she asked.

"You refused to watch the third one."

"I had an early class in the morning."

He was playing dirty. They'd made love on the couch in his dark living room with Boris Karloff stalking frightened virgins, and again as Lon Chaney turned into a werewolf.

"Tell me what you want," she said tensely.

"It's no big deal. All I need is the phone number of a woman named Matilda Merris. Your agency has done publicity for her art shows."

"Why do you want to contact her?"

"Marty Merris was her father."

"So? No one is interested in a baseball scandal that happened in the 1930s. Anyway, it doesn't sound like your kind of story."

Liv knew about Merris because she'd once been an avid baseball fan. Marty had been a Chicago Blues pitcher with a golden arm until he got caught taking money to throw a championship game. Billy's grandfather had had an interest in the team and tried to salvage the star pitcher's reputation to no avail. Matilda had remained loyal to the firm ever since.

"Mack Gallagher, my editor, wants Marty's name cleared. Merris's daughter is the only one who might be able to help. A couple of other *Post* reporters have struck out, but I don't intend to. I wrote a couple of letters to her without getting any response. I even went to her home in Saint Joseph, Michigan, but she let me stand out in the cold for hours without talking to me. I want to try to convince her on the phone, but I haven't been able to get her unlisted number."

"Why would your editor care after all this time?"

"Mack has a huge collection of Marty Merris

memorabilia. He wants to donate it to the new Chicago Museum of Sports when it opens in a year or so. The museum directors think Merris is too tainted to include."

"So you want to whitewash Marty Merris," she said.

"I only want to learn his side of the story. He refused to talk about it for the rest of his life. His daughter is in her seventies now, and she's the only one who can help clear his name."

"If it can be cleared," Liv said skeptically. "So your editor can donate his collection. He must think Marty is some kind of hero."

"Mack thinks he was the greatest pitcher of all time. It wouldn't hurt his reputation to be the man who had faith in Merris, not to mention the tax deduction if the museum accepts his memorabilia collection."

"I don't see how I can help you," Liv said.

"Just find Matilda's phone number in the agency files. Her last name is still Merris. She never married."

"I can't give you information from a client file. It's not ethical." She shook her head vehemently. "I just can't."

"I understand, but you're allowed to call clients, aren't you?"

He stood and put his hand on her wrist, a gesture as familiar as it was disturbing. Nick was a toucher, and his fingertips spoke a language all their own. She pulled away, afraid of the casual intimacy that came so easily to him. She couldn't let herself be attracted to him again, so she backed up a step and kept her eyes focused on a woman trudging by just beyond Nick's shoulder.

"All you have to do is ask permission to give me her number," he said. "You can explain as much or as little as you like."

"There has to be something wrong with that idea."

"What?" Nick arched his eyebrows. "Don't you think Matilda would like having her father's name cleared?"

"You don't know if it's even possible. Everyone thought he was guilty."

"Maybe there were extenuating circumstances," he suggested.

"I'll have to think about it. I can't make any promises."

"I understand, but remember, I'm not muckraking. If Merris deserves to be in the sports museum, he should be there."

"I'll think about it," she repeated unhappily.

"That's all I ask. Want me to walk you to your gate?"

"No, thank you. Just go."

Before she could move away, he brushed his lips against her forehead, almost but not quite kissing her. She felt an entirely different kind of shiver.

"Thanks for listening," he said softly, pressing his business card into her hand. "Call me at home or e-mail me at the paper. We'll work on your spontaneity problem."

Then he walked away, his bright red hood hanging between his shoulder blades and dark slacks hugging his muscular calves.

She hurried to the doors opening out to the tracks before he was out of sight. It was amazing how five years of separation seemed to dissolve, leaving her unwillingly attracted to Nick. She didn't want to think about him, but she was afraid he'd be back in her dreams.

TUESDAY MORNING the windchill was minus eleven. Liv had dressed for the weather in a knee-length brown skirt she'd had forever, a bulky cream sweater and high black boots with chunky heels. Not even Billy Lawrence could expect her to get frostbite by wearing a skimpy skirt on a day like this. At least that's what she thought until Brandi Jo came to work dressed in a black sleeveless sweater and red mini-skirt. Liv sent her to bring coffee from the employees' lounge.

"You don't outrank me yet," she said after the door closed behind the intern.

She tried to think of a job for Brandi Jo that would keep the little traitor out of action. Before she could come up with a chore so tedious the intern would beg to go home early, Boz barged into her office.

"Here's your coffee," he said with his usual over-the-top cheerfulness. "Hope you don't mind if I borrow Brandi Jo for a while. She didn't quite finish what I gave her yesterday."

Liv got up from the computer and took her mug with the Chicago Cubs logo from him. Now Ray Bosworth, a vice president, was delivering coffee because an intern had more important things to do.

"I don't need Brandi Jo," Liv said.

"Good, good. You know, Liv, that outfit isn't what I had in mind when I told you to loosen up."

"It's cold out, Ray, really cold." She clicked her teeth together for emphasis.

"Just keep it in mind," he said as he backed out the door.

For a moment she'd actually considered engineering an unfortunate accident with scalding coffee.

When had she turned into a bad-tempered shrew?

She winced because her head hurt every time she moved. She'd had a headache since she woke up, and it'd gotten worse when the frigid wind hit her face.

Her car had started, so she'd taken it as a sign not to call in sick. How could she beg off work because she'd had too much wine the night before?

Liv had too much work to waste time brooding. She had to send out press releases, then make a couple of urgent phone calls and find Matilda Merris's number, if she could bring herself to call her.

For the rest of the day Liv was glad to be overwhelmed by work so she didn't have time to think about her own problems. Every time she thought of looking up Marty's daughter, which was often since she couldn't seem to keep Nick out of her mind, she had something more pressing to do. Boz made five trips to her office between one and five o'clock and practically swamped her with jobs. Was he trying to overwork her so she would quit?

The security guard was doing the six o'clock lockup when Liv finally got to the lobby on her way home.

She hadn't found time to check on Matilda Merris, but she kept thinking about Nick in spite of her resolve to remain indifferent to him. He'd been the love of her life, the only man she'd wanted in her life forever. It had taken a couple years to get over him. Now he expected to breeze in and out of her life as if nothing had happened between them. Well, he had a surprise coming.

5

THE PHONE WAS RINGING when Liv got home. She dashed to get it on the kitchen extension and said a breathless "Hello."

"Hi, it's me," Amy said.

"I just got home. Can I call you back?" she asked.

"No, Sean and I are going out. I just wondered if we could get together sometime. I'd like to ask you a few questions about my wedding. Mom spaces out when I bring up anything about it."

"Sure, we can talk," Liv said with reservations.

"I can run over there Saturday morning. Talk to you then."

Liv agreed and hung up, then noticed the message light flashing on her answering machine. She pressed the play button.

"Just wondering if you had a chance to pull the Merris file. I'll get back to you."

Nick didn't identify himself. He didn't need to. She easily recognized his low, sexy voice, even distorted by her cheap answering machine.

Liv felt too drained by the demands of the day to

deal with Nick. Maybe later she'd call Dana for a good talk, but at the moment she felt too gloomy to inflict herself on anyone, let alone her best friend.

She went upstairs to check her e-mail messages, sitting in the swivel chair in front of her computer. It was her thinking spot, her comfort zone. She never felt alone when her fingers were on the keyboard.

Her first message was from her mother. Mom was excited about a makeover she'd had at an exclusive salon and casually mentioned she was staying at the house for now while Dad lived in a motel.

As soon as she'd checked all her messages, she sent a cheerful little note to her father's laptop computer hoping he was doing okay. She was too old to burden him with her problems, and he obviously had enough of his own.

She was startled when the phone suddenly rang. She picked it up, annoyed at herself for being so jumpy.

"Hi, it's Nick. Is it okay if I drop in on you?"

"Where are you?" She wanted to say an emphatic no, but she didn't want him to think she was spooked by his question.

"At the office. I can be there in less than an hour."

"I didn't have a chance to call Matilda Merris, so you'd be coming here for nothing."

"I have a few ideas about what you can say to her."

"My place is hard to locate." Her inner voice was screaming no, no, no, but her rational side wouldn't give in to panic. If Nick wanted to waste his time, she certainly wasn't afraid to see him. He couldn't sway her one way or the other anymore.

"The *Post* has a software program to find any address in the country," he said confidently. "See you soon."

The phone went dead in her ear. She couldn't stop him now unless she went out and tackled him in the snow on the way to her door. The real problem was that part of her wanted to see him again. She'd lost a friend as well as a lover when they parted. Seeing him again had made her feel that loss. They had had good times together, some of the best of her life, which only made her sense of loss worse.

About an hour later, she heard the buzzer. She smoothed her hair and tucked it behind her ears, then assured herself the nervous gesture had nothing to do with Nick's visit.

When she opened the door and saw Nick, she felt even more unsettled. Once, she'd lived to see him every day. Now she didn't know how she felt about him. Her anger had slowly ebbed over the years, but it had taken longer to get rid of the emptiness in her heart. Here he was, ruddy-cheeked from the cold with his parka unzipped and his hood off, indifferent to the near-zero temperature. She wanted to scold him about not dressing for the weather, but she wasn't his mother. She wanted to hug him to warm him up, but she wasn't his girlfriend—and never again would be. It took more than the ashes of an old relationship to start a new fire.

He came in carrying a big white paper sack, which he handed to her while he bent over to untie his laces.

"What is this?" she asked as he took off his wet suede boots and left them on the mat in front of the door.

"Chinese." He slipped out of his coat and hung it in her closet. "I'm hungry. Hope you haven't eaten." He knew she loved Chinese food, but she had to remember he was only being thoughtful so she'd help him with a story lead.

"Where do you want me to set up dinner, coffee table or kitchen?" he asked.

He took the sack from her and walked into the living room in his thick white crew socks.

"Neither," she said, dogging his footsteps to the kitchen.

He plunked the bag down on the yellow Formica tabletop. "Where are your plates?" He opened the wrong cupboard and took out a cereal box. "I see you've stayed hooked on my favorite, Choco-Crunchies."

She took the box away from him and returned it to the shelf. She remembered only too well how they used to tank up on cereal after making love in the morning.

"Once in a while I like a fast breakfast," she said primly.

"I'm glad I had some impact on your life," he teased.

Nick unwrapped two pairs of chopsticks while she set out two plates.

"I got your favorites, pepper steak and cashew chicken. Sweet-and-sour pork for me, but I'll share. Rice and egg rolls, of course," he said, putting more containers on the table. "And what would a Chinese dinner be without fortune cookies?"

She tried to pretend it was no big deal to have Nick in her kitchen. He looked more like his younger self in jeans and a red-and-blue-striped rugby shirt, but that didn't mean she wanted him there. In fact, it was a very bad idea. Her body was treacherous where Nick was concerned. Knowing him, though, the fastest way to get rid of him was to eat dinner and hope he had something else to do that evening.

They both started eating, using the chopsticks.

"Remember our rule," he said when she dropped a morsel of chicken on her sweater.

She remembered only too well. If either of them dropped food from the chopsticks, that person had to forfeit the piece of clothing it landed on. More than once they had finished a Chinese dinner in underwear or less and ended up in bed making leisurely love. "In your dreams," she said firmly.

"It was worth a try."

"You've wasted your time if you think I was kidding."

"About what?" He widened his eyes.

She knew that look of feigned innocence only too well.

"About having a strictly business relationship."

"If you mean no sex, say no sex. How are you going to loosen up if you're too shy to say it?"

"Nick, I do not want your help in changing my image. I maybe had a little too much wine last night when I suggested it."

He pushed aside his empty plate and stood, then walked into the living room without explanation. He returned in a minute with one of his reporter's notepads.

"I just happened to have this in my coat pocket," he said, turning a chair around to straddle it. "We're going to make a list for you. Isn't that what you like best, making endless lists?''

"They're not endless, and they serve a purpose,'' she said.

"You know once I get an assignment, I'm relentless,'' he said. "Unless you're not serious about our deal.''

"I don't need your help updating myself a little for my job.''

"Let's see what the fortune cookies say.'' Nick always changed the subject when he was losing an argument.

Liv remembered how Nick used to interpret the little snippets of prophecy. Somehow their advice always meant they should indulge in a few lusty hours in bed.

"Here, open yours first,'' he said, handing the cookie to her.

"Okay, but I'll interpret what it means for myself.''

She broke the hard little wafer cookie, extracted the thin slip of paper inside and read it silently.

"Let's hear it,'' he urged.

"It's just one of the usual silly sayings.''

"Olivia, let me see.'' He reached for the paper, but she didn't surrender it. "Please.''

"Okay, it's meaningless anyway.'' She read, "'You

are destined to do great things if you open your mind to possibilities.'"

"I like that," Nick said. "Here's mine. 'Friends are better than riches.'"

"That's all?"

"I think it says a lot. What kind of a friend would I be if I didn't help open your mind to possibilities?"

"I knew you'd make a big deal out of a fortune-cookie cliché."

"Okay, let's make our list."

He got up again and picked up the pencil she kept by the phone on the counter. One thing hadn't changed. Nick never could sit still for very long.

"Nick, I really don't need your help."

"I need yours, and we made a deal." He pulled a chair close to hers and sat. "Item number one—attitude."

"There's nothing wrong with my attitude."

"Denial," he said, writing that word in his hasty scrawl. "You can't change if you don't think it's necessary."

"Shouldn't I be lying on a couch, Dr. Matheson?" she asked.

"You're the one in trouble at work. You're trying to get out of this by starting a fight," he said, writing something she couldn't read.

"What's that word?" She leaned closer and peered at his list.

"Avoidance. You know you have a problem, but you're trying to avoid doing anything about it."

"That sounds like someone I used to know." She tucked her hair behind her ears.

"Stop fiddling with your hair. It's a dead give-away you're nervous about something. That brings me to the next point. Life doesn't always go as you planned. You can't be afraid of change. Throw away your master plan and enjoy life."

"I don't think you're qualified to psychoanalyze me."

"You're right. I'm not. Let's talk about image. That's really all your boss wants."

"Go home, Nick."

"I don't blame him. You're a gorgeous woman. Why hide that body?"

"Is that what you think I do?" She forced a weak laugh. "Look, how about we forget your part of the deal. I'll still contact Matilda Merris for you, but I really don't need your help."

"I should've known. You've gotten even more up-tight than you used to be," he said, seemingly unaffected by anything she said.

He came close and put his arm around her shoulders.

"We did have a good thing going for a while, didn't we?"

"I don't remember," she lied, stiffening as Nick rubbed her shoulder and upper arm. "Please stop that."

"Look," he said, "I really need your help on the Merris story. In exchange, I'll help you be more spontaneous. Is there anything wrong with mutual aid, cooperative compliance and a strictly business relationship?"

She wasn't convinced, but she did know Nick. He wasn't going to take no for an answer.

"Say what you were going to say, then go," she said.

"Don't make it sound like I'm going to trash you. You're beautiful, Liv." He stroked her cheek with his thumb.

"Please don't do that."

"A woman can buy enough hair dye to fill Lake Michigan without getting a shade as pretty as yours," he said, flicking her reddish-brown hair forward over one ear. "Why wear it in such a severe style?"

"I notice you cut yours shorter than ever."

"I spend a lot of time in locker rooms. I can't walk around looking like Goldilocks. But that's my point.

You need an image to fit your job. Take that skirt, for instance."

"I only wear it in cold weather."

"You had that wool sack in college."

"This conversation is demeaning and unhelpful. I was a little depressed when I asked for your help. I'm not now."

"I'm just trying to convince you not to dress like someone's grandmother. It's the attitude men pick up on, not just the clothes you wear. If you sincerely want to keep your job, it sounds to me as if you'll have to make some changes."

He was only saying what she already knew, but it hurt to hear it from him.

"Did you think that way when you dumped me?" She was not going to cry, she was not going to cry, she was not...

"No!" He practically choked on his denial. "I loved it that you were such a sweet person. But when you were naughty, you were incredible."

He slowly looked her over from head to toe. Liv knew she'd just been undressed by his bedroom eyes.

"If you use five percent of your latent powers to keep your job, no ambitious intern will squeeze you out. That's my contribution to your transformation."

"It really is time for you to leave."

She led the way to the door and took his coat out of the closet, making sure not to hold it close. Everything Nick wore carried a faint scent, as erotic as it was masculine. It would be disastrous to give in to her attraction to Nick. He really hadn't changed, and she didn't want to be spontaneous when it came to him. She could only get hurt if she allowed herself to want him again.

He took his coat, shrugged into it and left with a quick goodbye. She locked the door behind him.

OUTSIDE IN THE COLD, crisp air, Nick took a deep breath and tried to come down from a testosterone high that left his senses reeling. What had made him think he could be around Liv without feeling hot and bothered? She still turned him on like no one he'd ever met. Her clothes didn't even hint at the sensuous body under them, but he remembered only too well.

He'd had to clench his fists to keep from touching her. He knew what was hidden underneath—full, luscious breasts, shapely thighs, sleek hips and the warm, moist route to paradise.

He got in his car and debated whether to go back to her. No question he wanted to, but she'd deck him if he tried anything.

What was he thinking? He didn't want his life

complicated by an affair with Liv, and he wasn't enough of a jerk to love her and leave her a second time. Nothing was different between them. She was a planner, always looking for permanence and a happy ending. He wasn't any more ready for lasting ties than he had been five years ago.

He should go home, but he was too wired to sleep. Instead, he headed back downtown to the office. Kurt Michaels was pulling a late-nighter, but he'd probably be hungry later on. They could go out for a beer and a sandwich. Kurt was one of the few unmarried guys in the sports department, and they'd hit it off right away in spite of the competition between them to get the best assignments. Not only did Nick like Kurt, he could hang out with him without having to look at baby pictures or hear about plumbing repairs.

Maybe he'd been too hard on Liv. He was honest enough with himself to know he wasn't overly fond of change either. He liked to know where he stood and what his prospects were, but he avoided unnecessary upheavals. He wasn't as uptight as Liv, but he liked to plan ahead and know what his goals were.

Tonight he was lucky enough to find street parking. He rang the night bell, signed in with the security guard in the lobby and went up to the third-floor newsroom. He felt like talking but not about Liv.

"Hey, Nick, thought you went home for the night," Kurt called out from his desk.

"I have a couple things to wrap up. Wanna go out for a beer later?"

"Sure, if you can wait about forty-five minutes."

Kurt always sounded cheerful. It was a gift, one that made people overlook that the former football star had a razor-sharp mind. He had a round, guileless face and a brush cut that put players at ease. He got great interviews with athletes, but Nick knew he handled coaches and managers better.

He skimmed through his files on Merris while Kurt worked. Even though he was gregarious, Nick was self-contained. He didn't usually mind being alone, and he rarely dumped his problems on other people. But tonight he needed to talk, even if it was only about sports.

Liv Kearns was a threat. If he had any sense, he'd never go near her again. It would be a triumph if he nailed the truth about Marty Merris, but his career would survive if he didn't. Maybe there was another way to get to Matilda. His life would be much simpler if he didn't see Liv another time.

Much later he drove home on the freeway remembering the maze of roads lined with neat brick town houses where she lived. It was typical of the kind of place Liv would choose. Except for streetlights made to look like old-fashioned gaslights, everything in her development looked modern and efficient, a stark contrast to his apartment complex in Ira Heights. The builder there had tried to make the units different by using every material that could withstand a Midwestern winter, including wood, brick, stone, stucco and unidentifiable synthetics. The result was an architect's nightmare, but at least Nick never had any trouble finding his ground-level apartment. The rent was reasonable for suburban Chicago, and he could get to work in twenty minutes on a good day.

He had to pay close attention to slippery streets, but Liv remained in his thoughts all the way home. He wanted to help her, if only because he still didn't feel good about the way he'd dumped her. Maybe he had been too obsessed with making it to the top of his profession, but that wasn't the only reason he'd broken it off. He just hadn't been able to reconcile her idea of happiness, being together forever, with what he wanted from life. He didn't give himself high marks for maturity either. He had to know himself better before he could fully commit to a relationship, and Liv didn't deserve anything less.

She was still in his thoughts when he crawled into bed that night.

6

LIV GAVE BRANDI JO permission to leave early on Friday. In one week she'd be free of her. Whatever else happened, Liv was going to work as hard as possible to make sure she kept her job. If she ever did leave the firm, she wanted it to be her decision.

The office door banged open. If her status in the company weren't so precarious, she'd have a lock installed at her own expense.

"Liv, how's that little problem with Bushel going?" Boz asked.

A client who owned several Chicago-area restaurants had just lost a sexual harassment suit filed by one of his waitresses. Liv personally thought Arnie Bushel deserved to be strung up by his thumbs, but if his restaurants went bankrupt, a lot of jobs would be lost. She didn't have to like a client to do her job, but fortunately she didn't have to work with many macho dinosaurs like Bushel. His account, though lucrative to the firm, was her least favorite. She assured Boz everything was under control.

"One more thing, Liv," her boss said. "Since next

Friday is Brandi Jo's last day, I think we should do a little something for her. I thought a farewell luncheon in the office and a gift would be nice. Make the arrangements, would you?"

"Ray, couldn't we combine it with the office Christmas party? We can't possibly get a good caterer the week before Christmas. Every office in the city will be having a party."

"No, Brandi Jo has other plans for the twenty-third. See what you can do, Liv. It was Billy's idea."

Of course it was!

"Maybe I can order food from a deli."

"Do the best you can," Boz said as he left.

At least she hadn't had to deal with Nick since their Chinese dinner. She'd found Matilda Merris in the firm's records but hadn't had any success reaching her by phone. The woman didn't have an answering machine, unless it was turned off. Liv couldn't do anything else. She was much too busy to help Nick chase down a story.

Liv's immediate problem was planning a pitch to sign up a new client. Next week she was scheduled to meet with the owner of several Chicago clubs. She was still trying to figure out what to wear. Maybe one of Amy's castoffs would do since she didn't have time to shop for herself.

She heard the commotion of people going past her

closed door on their way home, but she had a few jobs yet to complete. It was past five-thirty when someone knocked.

"Come in," she called, expecting her visitor to be Dana on her way out.

"I waited in the lobby, but you didn't come down," Nick said, closing the door behind him.

"I'm just leaving for home." She stood and retrieved her purse from the file drawer, wishing he hadn't made her heart race by dropping in unexpectedly.

He slouched against the closed door, his squall jacket open and his hands thrust into the pockets of his jeans. Was he showing off his lean waist and flat belly, or was she reading too much into everything he did?

When he only watched her, she felt compelled to say something. "I found Matilda's file and called the number in it several times. She never answered the phone."

"You look nice," he said. Liv wanted to talk about Matilda, not about what she was wearing.

"Men like dresses. One zip, and they're off," he said as though she hadn't spoken. "No fumbling around with all the layers women pile on."

"There's nothing else I can do for you." Why did

she feel breathless and panicky? This was Nick, and he was nothing to her now.

"It's too long, but at least you look like a woman." He moved forward to block the way to her coat.

"You know I can't give out her phone number without her permission," Liv said impatiently. "Maybe she's out of town or something."

She had a terrible urge to look down at her charcoal wool sheath dress. Nick was studying it as though he intended to buy it—or remove it.

He advanced again and backed her up against the four-drawer file. She felt a handle press into her back.

The phone rang. She ignored it.

"Aren't you going to answer?" Nick asked.

"The office is closed."

"Here." He picked up the phone and handed it to her. "You never know when opportunity is on the other end."

"William Lawrence Associates. This is Liv Kearns," she said reluctantly, hoping it wasn't a client with an emergency.

"Miss Merris! Yes, I did call you earlier. It's so nice of you to call me back, especially since Dana usually handles your account."

"No, nothing to do with your art. There's a reporter at the *Chicago Post* who's very eager to talk to you about your father. He has the best of intentions."

Nick was standing directly behind her, trying to hear and at the same time resting one hand on her hip and the other on her waist. How did he expect her to concentrate?

"No, no, of course I would never betray your confidentiality by... No, absolutely not. I won't give out your phone number without your permission."

Nick slid one hand lower, kneading the fleshy part of her bottom. His free hand covered her fingers as she held the phone. She wanted to rap him on the knuckles with it, but it took all her concentration to make sense of what Miss Merris was saying.

"Yes, I absolutely promise," she said, startled when Nick put his hand on her thigh and gently squeezed it.

"But, Miss Merris, I'm sure the reporter I mentioned can be trusted. If you could give him a few minutes on the phone..."

His hand was between her thighs. She was going to kill him.

"He's more apt to believe you," Liv said, trying to persuade Matilda to give permission to give out her phone number, and at the same time squirming away from his hand.

Matilda Merris had a soft, pleasant voice, but she

was adamant in refusing to have anything to do with any reporter.

"Well, I'm really sorry I bothered you, Miss Merris. Thank you for calling."

"Why didn't you give me the phone?" Nick asked when she'd hung up. He stopped fondling her and sounded almost as irritated as she felt.

"She doesn't want to talk to you. You shouldn't—"

"Feel you up? Maybe I'm all wrong about what you should wear. That gray number is a real turn-on."

"Don't you have something to do or somewhere to go?"

"Not really." His face was so close she could smell mint on his breath.

"You didn't present my case to Matilda very well. You're definitely a naughty girl today."

"Nick, the cleaning service will be coming to clean my office. I have to leave."

She still tingled where Nick had stroked her. She had to get away before she let something really foolish happen.

"When will they get here?"

"Whenever! We shouldn't be here."

"Are you seeing anyone?" He put both hands on

her shoulders and studied her with an intensity that made her squirm.

"I...I see people."

"I didn't think you were," he said.

"Not everyone lives for sex."

He was poised to kiss her. How could she resist when she ached to be in his arms? Since his reappearance in her life, she couldn't stop thinking about how it would be to make love with him again. Was she losing her mind? This was Nick, the love-'em-and-leave-'em heartbreaker.

"I can't seem to get you out of my head." He didn't sound happy about it.

"I guess that means you're between women."

"You sell yourself short, Olivia."

"Put your coat back on. I'm leaving, and so are you."

"I really need to know something, Liv. It's been keeping me awake."

"Your insomnia has nothing to do with me."

"It has everything to do with you. Are you ever going to stop hating me?"

"I don't hate you."

She wasn't sure this was true. There was too much anger mixed up with the way she felt about Nick to analyze her feelings for him. She was at war with herself, wanting him to leave her alone and fearing that he actually would.

"Prove it," he said.

"Don't be silly."

"Kiss me."

"No! Why should I?" This was not good. What game was Nick playing?

"To prove you're indifferent to me. You'd kiss any guy who took you on a movie date, wouldn't you? A little peck is no big deal, so kiss me. Then we'll both know there's no spark left."

"You're right. Kissing you is no big thrill. I can prove that easily enough."

She stood on tiptoe and brushed her lips against his.

"That wasn't a kiss. You can do a lot better. Like this."

She closed her eyes as Nick's arms encircled her. His lips barely touched hers, but she couldn't help remembering the magic he could bring to a kiss.

She wasn't going to respond. He'd long ago forfeited the right to kiss her. When he failed to arouse her, he'd get the message.

He kissed with increasing pressure, exploring the corners of her lips then parting them with the tip of his tongue.

She'd stop him in a minute, but it wouldn't hurt to

enjoy herself just a little first. He was right. She hadn't been properly kissed in quite a while. His tongue caressed the roof of her mouth and reminded her of other things Nick could do with it. He held her so close her breasts flattened against the hard expanse of his chest, but she wanted to be held even tighter. Her fingers wandered over his shirt, then she locked her arms around his waist.

He put his hands on either side of her head and kissed her forehead, eyelids and the tip of her nose. He was trying to be playful, but this was no game. She felt cold air and realized he'd lowered her dress zipper to expose her back.

"Haven't you proved your point?" she asked, her voice muffled by the persuasive pressure of his mouth on hers.

His hands warmed her back with soft rhythmic strokes, and she was too dazed to remember what his point was.

"Let me," he said, lowering her dress over her shoulders and down to her waist with her arms still captured in the long sleeves. He pushed aside the cups of her bra and lowered his head.

She couldn't stop him because she couldn't stop herself. His breath was warm against her skin, but she shivered as his tongue moistened and teased her nipple.

The phone rang again. This time he urged her to ignore it, but she reached for the receiver to give herself time to think about what they were doing.

"Hello." Her voice cracked.

"Liv, are you all right?"

It was Dana. She'd forgotten her promise to meet her best friend in the lobby. Dana had left early to run some papers to a client and had come back especially so they could have an after-work drink.

"Oh, Dana, I'm so sorry! I got involved in a project and forgot all about time."

"Don't beat yourself up," her friend said. "I'll give you a rain check, but I think I'd better head for home. There's a winter-storm watch. My mom will be calling my apartment every ten minutes if it starts to snow to make sure I get home."

"I'm really sorry," Liv said. She was also chilly standing naked to the waist. Apparently they turned down the heat when everyone left. She wiggled back into her dress.

"Yeah, you said that—three times. No problem, but you'd better leave now. Are you alone up there?"

"Not exactly. I'll see you Monday." She hung up before Dana could ask more questions.

"You had a date?" Nick asked.

He was sitting in her swivel chair, his legs outstretched and his shirt unbuttoned to the waist. He reached out to pull her down onto his lap, but she backed away, knowing exactly what he had in mind. If he thought the sight of his manly chest would make her crazy with lust, he was right. But if he thought she'd let this go any further, he was dead wrong.

"You made me forget I was supposed to meet a friend," she said.

She was hot and wet between her legs, aching to go to him but scared of how easily he could make her want him. If she were wound up any tighter, she'd burst, but she couldn't let herself give in to Nick's overwhelming sensuality. It could only lead to heartbreak. She couldn't bring herself to have casual sex with this man no matter how desperately her body craved it.

"Sorry about your friend," he said. "Sit on my lap. Please."

"We're not going to do that," she said. "You've proved I don't hate you. I just dislike you intensely and never want to see you again."

Her mouth was dry, and her lips felt chapped and sore. Her cheeks were burning as much from embarrassment as from her feverish denial of a very basic need. How could she let Nick do this to her? How could she let down her guard with Matheson, of all men?

"I can't give you very high marks on spontaneity," he said, lazily buttoning his shirt and tucking it into places she wouldn't be going, not tonight or ever. "I don't suppose you'll give me Matilda's number?"

"Is that why—" She was so stunned, she sputtered.

"No. I didn't come on to you for a phone number. You always sell yourself short. Any heterosexual male with a normal libido would want to have sex with you. But I give up for now. Can I walk you to the lobby?"

"No, please, just go."

"Sorry I messed up your date."

"It wasn't a date. Dana had to get home anyway. It's snowing like mad."

"I could drive you home." He had his coat on, poised to leave.

She wanted to stay with him, and it scared her. Maybe she was a control freak, but Nick was throwing her off balance, big time. He made her feel alive and sexy, but she vividly remembered the way he'd let her down five years ago. She absolutely would not risk being hurt that badly again.

"Goodbye, Nick." She said it with a finality she meant.

7

NICK BRACED HIMSELF as sharp needles of cold water stung his back. He shuddered under the punishing spray but refused to step out from under it until he'd completely negated Liv's effect on him. He gave up two degrees short of hypothermia, turned off the water in the shower and roughly toweled himself dry.

Talk about bad ideas! He should've called Liv instead of cornering her alone in the office. He'd thought he was being discreet, following a lead on the Merris story without letting anyone at William Lawrence Associates know she was helping him contact a former client.

He hurried into the bedroom and grabbed a pair of sweatpants from a drawer, hastily pulling them on. He didn't begin to warm up until he pulled on his green terry-cloth robe and thrust his feet into his leather bedroom slippers.

He'd temporarily subdued his libido, but he couldn't forget how Liv had turned him on. In his imagination he could still taste her lips and feel his tongue on her luscious nipples.

What had he been thinking? He hadn't gone to her office intending to seduce her. They had a stick-to-business arrangement. He was a hundred percent in favor of a hands-off rule with Liv, but unfortunately he found her eminently touchable. Her style of dressing didn't turn him off in the least, maybe because he had such a good memory. He knew what she was hiding under her clothes.

He'd loved her firm, strong legs wrapped around him and the fullness of her breasts under his hands. Her body was sleek and agile, all that any man could wish for and her face was achingly beautiful.

He smiled at the memory of their first lovemaking. Liv had been a little shy—no, a whole lot shy. She'd wanted to undress under the sheet. It had taken a lot of persuasion to make her believe that her body was too gorgeous to hide. He felt hot just thinking about how eager he'd been to peel away the layers of her clothing.

The affair may have started off slow, but Liv had surprised him more than once. She could be as wild in bed as she was restrained and proper out of it. For her sake, he hoped that hadn't changed. She'd been crazy about sex in their time together. He'd hate it if he'd done anything to dull her enthusiasm, but she was hard to read. Was she piling on clothes to hide her sexuality? Had she lost confidence in herself as a woman and sex partner?

There was no point in remembering how fantastic Liv had been. He'd made a dumb move in her office, and she'd shot him down exactly as he deserved. He'd blown his chance to be with her five years ago, and no woman was likely to forgive rejection.

He wandered into the kitchen area of his efficiency apartment and surveyed the fridge for dinner possibilities, but food wasn't the main thing on his mind. He knew why his time with Liv had been so memorable. It was more than sleeping together. He'd cared about her so much it had unnerved him, but he hadn't been able to buy into her idea about a permanent relationship. Why couldn't two people bond and enjoy each other without rings, vows and promises they might not be able to keep?

Without giving it too much thought, he slapped together a sandwich, grabbed a beer from the back of the otherwise empty bottom shelf of the fridge and carried his meal to the living room.

He wasn't a slob by nature, but he didn't spend enough time in his apartment to care much how it looked. The decor, such as it was, was pretty much generic-rental boring, white walls, gray carpeting flecked with black and white, and vertically slatted blinds on the windows and sliding glass door that led to a minuscule weed patch in back. His one concession to comfort was an oversize brown leather couch, purchased after he moved to Chicago. He liked to stretch out full length and watch the Eternal Sports Network, as one ex-girlfriend had called it.

Why couldn't a man and woman have fun without sticky relationship problems? Everyone knew marriage was like a lottery. Only a few lucky people struck it rich. Being married hadn't worked for his parents, and they were both decent, unselfish people.

He'd seen friends try the happily-ever-after bit, too. They'd been having fantastic hot sex with the women of their dreams, then they'd bought a ring and things started to change. Pretty soon they were arguing with their spouses about where to live, how to spend their money and who should take out the trash. Then divorce lawyers latched onto the women, and his friends' futures degenerated into endless bickering and support payments.

When did he get so cynical? He liked his life just the way it was. He didn't want Liv or any other woman to change it. If his editor sent him to cover the Super Bowl, the NBA playoffs or even the Olympics, he could go without guilt about neglecting a significant other.

What he needed was a no-strings woman who was as committed to her work as he was. Maybe he should start something with the "Chicago Today" editor at the *Post*. She was a few years older than he was and a little thin for his taste, but she'd tried marriage twice and didn't have any romantic illusions. He'd gotten a few signals from her. He wasn't opposed to convenient sex if both parties got something out of it.

Or maybe he was kidding himself. He snorted with self-disgust and carried the remains of his meal back to the kitchen. The cold shower had worn off, and images of Liv were sneaking into his consciousness.

Why hadn't she decked him tonight? If she wanted him as much as he wanted her, they were in big trouble. No way could he reconcile the lust he was feeling with her vulnerability. He didn't want to hurt her again, but the only way to avoid it was to avoid her.

He would stay away from her as soon as he wrapped up the Merris story. His editor was pressuring him to get something that would make the sports museum directors include the black-sheep player's memorabilia in their collection. Aside from battering down Matilda's door and getting himself arrested, he didn't know a way to get a response from her without using Liv.

Maybe he should call Liv and apologize. He found his cell phone and punched in her number from memory, then had second thoughts after the first ring. He hung up feeling cowardly, but what could he say to her?

He couldn't apologize, because he wasn't sorry for anything. It hadn't been smart to come on to her and get both of them heated up. He could confess to being immature and unwise, but there was nothing adolescent about the way he wanted Liv. What he didn't want was a house in the suburbs, two kids and a slobbering dog. Liv had tempted him once to forget his reservations about commitment.

Maybe he'd take another cold shower.

LIV WOKE UP Saturday morning feeling hot from too many covers and sexy from too much Nick Matheson. Someday when she had more time, she had to read up on female sexuality. Why did she go for weeks, even months, perfectly content with her chaste state, then turn into wild-woman with a brushfire smoldering inside her? Whenever she thought she could be content living the life of a nun, something happened to shake her up. This time Nick had happened.

She crawled out from under her insulated blanket and comforter and searched for her fluffy yellow slippers with her toes. What did she have to do today? She wished life was like a ball of modeling clay, easy to mold into any shape she liked. Lately hers was a labyrinth of tunnels and pitfalls. Whenever she had a handle on everything she should be doing, she was sidetracked by some new problem. She needed a four-day weekend just to organize her thoughts.

She liked to be able to handle everything that came her way, but too much had been thrown her way all at once. Her parents' divorce was hard enough to accept, but it also meant Amy would rely on her to pull the wedding together. Then she had a tricky situation at work, one she might not be able to solve in her usual style—working harder and longer. If Billy Lawrence really wanted to replace her, she had the battle of her life on her hands. She had to prove she was invaluable to the firm. She liked her job too much to give it up without a fight.

Then there was Nick. This was the worst possible time for him to reappear in her life, not that any time would be good. She had to concentrate on all the chaos around her, but he was throwing her off.

How could she concentrate on anything after he'd inserted himself into her life again? Matilda Merris didn't want to talk to him. Why couldn't he accept rejection? Liv had, and it hurt a lot more to lose a lover than it did to fail at a story.

Her life was racing out of control, and there was nothing she hated more. One way or another, she was going to get a grip on her problems and work through them. She didn't have the time or energy to worry about what Nick wanted.

She ignored a little voice in her head that wondered if he wanted her again. But it didn't really matter what he thought. Nothing was going to happen between them.

She sat on the edge of the bed with one slipper on her foot and one still to be found. Boz didn't care if she spent Saturday chasing around to organize a luncheon for the treacherous intern. He had a wife to do his laundry, clean his home and shop for groceries. As far as she could tell, all he did around the office was run Billy's errands and make her life miserable.

Was she turning into a whiner? She got down on her hands and knees, found the missing slipper and remembered her sister. Amy was coming over at ten, which gave Liv about forty minutes to transform herself into a cheerful, sympathetic sister.

It was natural for siblings to get together in times of crisis, but usually Liv would do the consoling even though her sister had Sean. Liv felt a little guilty, but she wasn't in the mood to hear any complaints from Amy. Her sister was having regular sex. She wasn't tied up in knots because she wanted someone who was not emotionally available. Amy drifted through life and let the good things happen. Liv planned, organized and worried about bad things like falling in love with Nick again.

"Oh, no!" she said aloud.

How could she even think of Nick that way? She already knew he hadn't changed in any way since their time together.

Hurrying into the bathroom, she turned on the cold water in the shower stall and let her long white flannel nightgown fall in a heap on the floor. She stepped under the icy needles of spray expecting to suffer, and shrieked in agony for less than two seconds before she ducked out.

Cold showers must be some kind of guy joke, she thought, frantically turning on the hot water for a nice warm scrub. Her cold tap water couldn't be more than a degree above freezing. It had hurt more than a snowball in the face.

Okay, now she was fully awake and rational. Maybe for a short while she would go to sleep thinking about Nick and wake up wishing he was with her, but this time she'd get over him in a hurry. She could control her daytime thoughts, and he wasn't going to creep into them. He was history. Any woman who allowed herself to get obsessed with one unavailable guy was a woman who'd lost control of her own life. Liv did not intend to let that happen to her. If anything did develop between them, which was unlikely, she'd call the shots and direct the action. It would only happen if she wanted it.

BY THE TIME Amy got there, Liv felt more like herself.

"I don't know what I'm going to do," Amy said the second she stepped into Liv's town house. "I wish I could handle things the way you do."

Liv kindly didn't mention that her sister was the one who was planning a wedding and a wonderful future with the man she loved.

"What's wrong?" Liv dutifully asked, hanging up her sister's shearling coat and scarf.

Amy dressed in ultrafeminine pastels. She kept her hair, naturally lighter than Liv's, tinted honey blond with soft waves around her face. She wasn't cuddly-cute like Brandi Jo, but she'd inherited the best features from both sides of the family, including a cute little nose, high cheekbones and perfect teeth. Liv was the first to admit Amy was the pretty one, but she did enjoy being two inches taller than her sister.

"Life," Amy said.

"Let's have some coffee. I haven't had breakfast yet."

Amy prefaced every conversation with drama ever since she got engaged. She wouldn't get to her real reason for being there until she'd had a chance to emote.

Liv had coffee ready, so it was only a minute before they were seated at the kitchen table with cups of hot black hazelnut decaf.

"I talked to Mom," Liv said. "But I haven't heard a word from Dad." She didn't realize until she said it how much that hurt.

"He spent three days holed up in a motel room with the flu. Mom told me. He was too stubborn to bother getting a flu shot, of course. I guess they still talk. You know, about dividing things and divorce stuff."

"Is he okay now?" Liv asked.

"I guess. It's hard to keep Mom on track when we're talking."

"She has a lot on her mind." Liv suddenly realized she was famished. "Want some toast?"

"Sure, why not? I dashed out without a bite. I have loads of things to do today, and I have to go to the shop and make up a special centerpiece with yellow roses for a fiftieth wedding anniversary tomorrow. Can you imagine being married to the same person for fifty years? What do people talk about after that long?"

"No idea," Liv said, putting four slices of bread in her toaster oven.

"I'm almost afraid to ask," Amy said, "but did you get all the calls made to cancel the party?"

"Yes." The less said about that the better, although Liv anticipated her sister's next question.

"How did Nick react?"

"He took it like a man," Liv said.

"He got mad?"

"No, of course not, but he didn't like the message I left on his answering machine. I was a little abrupt."

"How do you know he didn't like it? Did he call you back?"

"No, he came to the office."

"He came to your office? That sounds interesting."

"It was only by chance. He didn't even know I worked there. He was hoping to contact one of the firm's clients, Matilda Merris, for a story. Her father was a baseball player who was involved in a big scandal."

Sports and history were outside Amy's sphere of interests, so Liv didn't elaborate.

"So did you help him?"

"I couldn't divulge confidential information, but I called her. She wants nothing to do with reporters."

Amy laughed softly. "When did Nick Matheson ever take no for an answer?"

"He'll have to this time."

"You're not mad because I invited him to the party, are you? I just thought—"

"I know exactly what you thought. Good try, but please don't play matchmaker again, okay? If I ever find someone, he'll be more reliable than Nick."

She stood watching the bread through the glass door because the timer wasn't very reliable on the old appliance. She liked her toast golden brown but not dried out or burnt around the edges. Was being fussy about food the first indication she was becoming too set in her ways? Was she turning into a cartoon-character spinster? When the toast was perfect, she slid the slices onto plates, then spread them with margarine and sprinkled on cinnamon sugar from a glass shaker. Amy watched without saying much.

Liv sat down and started eating with an appetite, remembering she'd forgotten to eat dinner.

Amy nibbled her toast listlessly, then laid it down and watched Liv finish hers. "I'm getting nervous about the wedding," Amy said. "Marriage is such a fragile thing. People do it, then they undo it. Mom doesn't even seem interested in mine anymore."

"She's just preoccupied by the divorce," Liv said, hoping she was right. She didn't know how her parents felt about Sean, but she thought he was a little loud and show-offish. Of course, Amy always did like extroverts. He had a good job selling medical supplies, and a salesman couldn't be quiet and shy.

"Sometimes I think we're in a rut already." Now Amy sounded really worried. "What will happen after we're married? Can you be too comfortable with the man you love?"

Too comfortable? Liv mused. She'd never been completely comfortable with Nick, not even in college when she'd thought she'd loved him.

"I'm probably being silly," Amy said before Liv could think of any way to reassure her sister. "It's just prewedding nerves. I have so many decisions to make, and all Mom wants to talk about is her divorce. I don't need to know who gets the dining-room set. I don't care if they sell the leaded-glass lamp. I was always afraid I'd be the one to break it. I have problems of my own."

"It will get better." Liv wanted to comfort her sister, but her words sounded pretty lame.

She couldn't offer Amy much comfort when her own belief in happily-ever-after marriages had taken such a blow. Maybe her parents would be happier apart. They'd married young and grown a lot in nearly thirty years. Liv could admit now that she hadn't been ready for a permanent relationship five years ago, no matter how much she'd loved Nick.

"Well, I have to go," Amy said. "Will you help me out a little on the wedding? I never dreamed it would be so complicated."

"You know I will." Liv felt more resignation than enthusiasm as she followed her sister to the door.

"Oh, before I forget," Amy said when she had her coat on. "Sean and I are going to his parents' house in Milwaukee for Christmas. They invited Mom to come too. She hasn't said for sure whether she'll go, but she probably will. Christmas wouldn't be much fun at the family homestead, would it? I guess you can get together with Dad, can't you?"

"I guess. Keep me posted," Liv said.

"Christmas," she said when the door closed behind her sister. She'd been too busy to finish her shopping. It was unlikely she'd send cards since she hadn't bought any. Her artificial wreath and three-foot tree were still boxed up in the garage, and they could stay there for all the holiday spirit she had. Now she had to worry about the logistics of celebrating the day.

There was only one way she really wanted to spend Christmas, but it would never happen. No matter how naughty or nice she was, Santa wouldn't put Nick in her stocking.

8

WHAT WAS THE WORST that could happen? Nick wondered as he parked his Tracker in the driveway leading to Liv's single-car garage. He had reservations about seeing her again, but he couldn't shake the feeling that he'd behaved badly in her office yesterday.

Was he developing an overly active conscience? Talk about a career handicap! In his profession he had to be as self-confident and aggressive as any top athlete, interviewing coaches and players with lousy attitudes. He seldom apologized for anything.

He stared at Liv's bright green front door pondering what his reception would be. No doubt she'd think he was there because of the Merris story, but he didn't plan to mention Matilda, not today anyway. He'd come as a friend. Sure, he knew ex-lovers didn't become bosom buddies, but he didn't want Liv to hate him.

He walked to her door rehearsing what to say. Even if she didn't boot him out, she certainly wouldn't be thrilled to see him. He'd forfeited the right to put his hands on her five years ago.

When he pressed her doorbell, it made a buzzing noise that carried through the door. Maybe she was out shopping. His watch showed it was only 11:37. He had nearly seven hours before he had to cover a hockey game, but he didn't want to spend them waiting for her to get home.

Suddenly, the door opened, and there was Liv in jeans and a faded blue sweatshirt, her feet encased in thick gray socks. He found her eyes dark and enticing, even as she raked them over him in unspoken disapproval.

"Hi," he said. "I was in the neighborhood."

She arched one eyebrow, giving him a skeptical look that challenged him to come up with a better story.

"Well, not really. I put my car on autopilot, and this is where it brought me."

"Do you have a reason why I should let you come in?" she asked.

"You're losing heat with the door open. Hate to see you cool off your whole place while we talk."

"What do we have to talk about?" She wasn't going to be easy.

"I'll leave the minute you want me to. Promise." He held up his palms in a gesture of peace.

"Oh, all right. Come in if you must."

She turned and walked into the living room while he stood just inside the door trying to come up with a good reason for being there. Even in a baggy shirt and old faded jeans, she devastated him. If they ever had a contest for the world's most beautiful butt, she'd be a contender. Did she know how she affected men when she swayed her hips like that? Knowing Liv, she didn't have a clue.

"Well?" She turned and faced him from what she probably considered a safe distance. "Why are you here?"

"I want you to do something spontaneous…"

Where had that come from? He should know better than to open his mouth when his brain wasn't fully engaged.

"What?" At least he had her attention.

"A mystery trip, something completely unplanned and fun. Isn't that what you need, more spontaneity in your life?"

The biggest mystery was where he was going to take her if she agreed to go. There wasn't much chance of that, though. She'd wrinkled her nose at his suggestion, a familiar gesture he'd always thought was cute.

"Go someplace with you now? Does this have anything to do with Merris?"

"Absolutely nothing," he assured her.

"But you won't tell me now what you have in mind?"

"No, that's why it's a mystery trip."

"You don't think I'll go, do you? You've only asked because your one-track mind is positive I'll say no. Then you can say, 'See, you don't know how to be spontaneous.'"

One-track mind? If she really knew what was buzzing in his brain, she'd slap his face. He was there because he couldn't stay away. It didn't make sense after all that had happened between them, but he wanted to be with her. His choice would be to spend the day in bed, but he'd settle for whatever he could get.

"All right, I'll go. Help yourself to coffee while I change. The pot is still hot."

She went up carpeted stairs without a backward glance. No woman he'd ever known changed clothes without knowing where she was going. Liv had given in too easily. What was she up to?

He shrugged out of his coat, dropped it on the couch and went into the kitchen. There were two coffee cups on the table, one smeared on the rim with pink lipstick. Liv wasn't wearing any, so she must have had a friend over or maybe her sister.

He rinsed the dregs out of the cup Liv had used,

filled it with coffee and added some milk from the fridge. It was good, but Liv did practically everything well. He didn't understand why she was still unattached. The men in Chicago couldn't be so blind.

He sat and sipped coffee, considering where to take her. This was Chicago, entertainment capital of the Midwest. He should be able to come up with something.

Women loved Woodfield Mall. It was good for hours of wandering, but did he want to stand around in women's shops while she checked out racks and shelves of girlie stuff? Not exactly, but he wanted to be with Liv badly enough to suggest a sure winner. Anyway, with Christmas so close, she might have gifts to buy. He decided to go for it.

He finished his coffee, got up and rinsed both cups. Liv liked things tidy; he could be tidy. What he didn't know was why he was trying so hard. It wasn't about Matilda Merris. He didn't want Liv to feel used. After all, there wasn't any reason why two old friends couldn't continue to be friendly. Liv was sweet, caring and funny. Sure, she sometimes got uptight when things didn't go her way, but she'd helped him a lot when his parents were divorcing. The least he could do was give her some support until she came to terms with her parents' breakup.

She walked up behind him as he was putting the cups on the drain board.

"I'm ready. Now, where are we going?"

He took in her navy cords and yellow crewneck sweater. It suited her vision of herself, but he knew what her boss meant about loosening up. She was hiding her assets. There was nothing wrong with a beautiful woman dressing to look even better.

"How about Woodfield Mall?" he asked.

"Good choice."

She marched, literally, to the closet and pulled out a long dark coat. It covered way too much of her, but this was frigid Chicago. He'd worked on both coasts, in Boston and San Francisco, and he was definitely a California kind of guy. Too bad the best career opportunity he'd ever had was in Chicago, his home turf, but he didn't regret finding Liv again. Maybe someday he'd get another opportunity to better himself in sunny climes, all the more reason to stay unattached.

He picked up his coat and put it on as they walked out. He didn't know where this was going, but he felt inordinately pleased to be spending a day with Liv.

9

NICK HELD THE DOOR for her, and Liv got into his surprisingly practical small SUV, not at all like the
snazzy vintage Mustang he'd been so proud to drive
in college.

"What happened to your Mustang convertible?"
she asked.

"I needed something more reliable." He didn't
sound happy about it. "Besides, it would've been a
crime to bring that little beauty back to salty roads
after I had her completely restored. She's better off
in California."

"*It's* better off in California," Liv said.

It was an old disagreement. She thought it was
silly to assign gender to inanimate objects. Nick insisted on personifying his vehicles.

"*I* was better off in California," he said, sounding
a little regretful, "but my job there didn't have any
future."

Liv buckled her seat belt and was pleased to see
Nick did too. He'd been pretty reckless when they
were together.

"I know why you're doing this," she said.

If they were going to have a big fight, she might as well start it close to home in case she wanted to walk back.

"You only think you do," he said.

"You want more help with Matilda Merris," she said. "You think you can persuade me by being nice."

"Can I?" He sounded indifferent.

"No, but you're welcome to try."

"You called Matilda for me, and she said no. There are other stories." He shrugged as much as he could while driving.

Nick giving up on a story? She wasn't convinced, but she was curious. If she didn't know better, she might think this was a date.

"How's your sister taking the divorce?" he asked after a long silence. "I cleverly deduced that the second cup on the table was hers. Pink lipstick."

She was beginning to be sorry she'd accepted his offer. She wasn't spontaneous, and Saturday was a badly needed catch-up day. She'd planned to do a dozen little chores, not to mention find a caterer for Brandi Jo's luncheon. It didn't usually bother her to see people get ahead in the profession. Brandi Jo was an exception. A *big* exception.

"Yes, Amy came over this morning. Mostly she's

NO POSTAGE
NECESSARY
IF MAILED
IN THE
UNITED STATES

BUSINESS REPLY MAIL

FIRST-CLASS MAIL   PERMIT NO. 717-003   BUFFALO, NY

POSTAGE WILL BE PAID BY ADDRESSEE

HARLEQUIN READER SERVICE
3010 WALDEN AVE
PO BOX 1867
BUFFALO NY 14240-9952

Get FREE BOOKS and a FREE GIFT when you play the...

LAS VEGAS
GAME

Just scratch off the gold box with a coin. Then check below to see the gifts you get!

YES! I have scratched off the gold Box. Please send me my **2 FREE BOOKS** and **gift for which I qualify**. I understand that I am under no obligation to purchase any books as explained on the back of this card.

▼ DETACH AND MAIL CARD TODAY! ▼

342 HDL DUYP   142 HDL DUY5

FIRST NAME	LAST NAME

ADDRESS

APT.#	CITY

STATE/PROV.	ZIP/POSTAL CODE

(H-T-03/03)

Visit us online at www.eHarlequin.com

7	7	7	Worth TWO FREE BOOKS plus a BONUS Mystery Gift!
🍒	🍒	🍒	Worth TWO FREE BOOKS!
🔔	🔔	☘	TRY AGAIN!

Offer limited to one per household and not valid to current Harlequin Temptation® subscribers. All orders subject to approval.

worried about her wedding. Mom's been too busy to help, so she's panicking. But she'll be fine eventually."

"Will you?" He surprised her by sounding as if he really cared.

Did Nick feel sorry for her? Was he taking a poor lonely girl on an outing to cheer her up? She'd rather be tricked into a surprise visit to Matilda than have him treat her as a charity case.

"I'm fine," she said. "My parents are capable of doing what's best for them. I have my own life."

Did she sound too defensive? Did it matter what Nick thought? Was he trying to pay her back for her sympathy during his parents' divorce problems? She hated the idea that he might feel he owed her something.

He turned on the wipers because snowflakes were melting on the windshield. For a minute she hadn't been paying attention to anything outside the car.

"I have to cover a hockey game tonight," Nick said, "but we have the whole afternoon to shop. I have to buy a few Christmas presents myself."

When they reached the crowded parking area of the mall, he had to cruise around to find a spot. Half of Chicago seemed to have flocked out to the giant shopping center. They walked through the lot with their arms linked. The sky was leaden gray, but the

light snowfall was more picturesque than threaten-
ing. It reminded her of snowmen and snow angels,
the fun things she'd made in the winter when she
was a kid. She finally felt relaxed with Nick, pretty
sure he didn't have any self-serving motive for taking her to the mall.

She could feel the power in his biceps, even
through their heavy coats. His strength was part of
his appeal, and she felt especially vulnerable to it.
Once, he'd easily scooped her into his arms and carried her to his bed. Her throat ached thinking about
all the lost nights going to bed alone instead of with
Nick. She was shocked to realize she was lonely. She
was blessed with a loving family, good friends and
pleasant co-workers—with a few notable excep-
tions—but they were no substitute for one special
person to love.

The oddest thing about this trip was Nick's reason
for bringing her here. Why did he want to be with
her if he wasn't eager for more help with Matilda
Merris?

Big fluffy snowflakes fluttered over the people
coming and going, softening the commercial setting.
When nothing else came to mind, there was always
the weather to talk about.

"I love walking in the snow," she said.

"You always did." He said it absentmindedly.

"So you do remember some things we did together?"

Old friends should reminisce about things they'd shared. She didn't want their past to be forbidden territory. She didn't see how she could spend a whole day with him pretending there had never been anything between them.

"I remember everything," he said. "You were sweet and insecure..."

"Insecure?" They walked into the mall concourse, and she pulled away from him.

"Okay, a little shy, a little repressed."

"Thanks a lot."

"That was when we first met. Not later."

He grinned broadly and defused her anger. "I'm kidding. You were right to rein me in sometimes. For instance, we could've been kicked out of the university for having sex in the provost's garden shed. I just couldn't resist that silly miniature barn."

"Or the library stacks. Or the parking garage. Or..."

"We had a good time, didn't we?"

She couldn't deny that, but she wasn't going to admit it either. She was in grave danger of falling in love with him again, and that would be disastrous.

He took her hand in a warm, firm grip, and she allowed herself to pretend they were together again.

He looked down at her, his blue eyes hazy and unreadable. She knew he wanted to kiss her, but she was glad he didn't. A noisy, crowded mall was no place to rekindle old feelings, not that she wanted that to happen.

Her trip down memory lane was unsettling. She remembered that one of the truly marvelous things about Nick was the wonderful taste of his mouth. She'd never understood it, but he tasted delicious. She could recall the tickle of his breath on her skin and the flick of his eyelashes against her closed lids when he'd kissed her tenderly. But some memories should be put aside permanently.

"So, where should we go first?" he asked. "I guess if you can't find what you want here, it doesn't exist."

"I need gifts for my father, mother and sister. It's only ten days until Christmas, so I'd better do all my shopping today. And I need a new outfit for the office Christmas party."

"Think of me as your personal shopper."

"You hate shopping."

"Not with you."

THE HUGE MALL had a store for everyone. One concourse had a prefab home fully assembled and furnished. Another had a Christmas tree that rivaled the White House's. Nick soon lost track of the number of stores they checked out, and he was carrying the packages to prove it. Liv's Christmas list was as long as Santa's, and she liked to check the same item in a couple of stores before buying it.

Oddly enough, he was enjoying himself, and it had everything to do with Liv. He wanted to be with her regardless of what they were doing. He wasn't sure this was a good idea, but she was becoming important to him again. He didn't want to hurt her again, but he was like an addict, needing to see her one more time then finding it wasn't enough.

When her Christmas gift shopping was finally out of the way, she began searching for a new dress for the party. When she disappeared into a department store changing room, he resigned himself to hanging around and waiting. No matter where he stood, he seemed to be in the way of other shoppers or blocking a clothing rack or aisle. He'd wanted to follow Liv into the little room where she was trying on the dress, but she didn't give him a chance. Instead, he was out in the store jockeying for a spot to wait and imagining her in panties and bra pulling on the hot little red dress he'd encouraged her to try.

She came out at last and found him backed against a rack of dresses.

"I'm going to buy it for the Christmas party," she said.

"Good choice."

"I don't know why I'm bothering. It isn't as if the party is a big deal or anything."

"Does that mean you don't have a date?" he asked.

"I don't need a date." Her tone was a little too vehement.

"When is it?"

"The Tuesday before Christmas. If it's anything like last year's, some people will party all day, but the party officially starts at three o'clock."

"I happen to be free that afternoon." He tried to sound casual, not that he was crazy about office parties. He just didn't like the idea of Liv fending off a bunch of drunken PR men.

She paid for the dress without responding to his hint. Hell, it was more than a hint. A little voice in his head was saying, "Choose me, choose me."

When had he ever waited to be asked?

"I'll meet you there a little after five," he said.

"I don't think that's a good idea."

"I'll be your designated driver."

"Really, Nick, the party is not a big deal. Thanks, but I can get home on my own."

"You shouldn't take a train that late at night," he pointed out.

"There are several people who can give me a ride, or maybe I'll drive myself."

She started walking out of the store carrying her new dress in a purple-and-silver sack.

"How about some lunch?" He'd convince her about the party later. It was nearly three, and he was ravenous.

"I have one more thing to buy first."

He didn't moan or groan, but only because shopping with her was better than not being with her at all. He might be in big trouble here. She was making him feel the way he did at the top of a roller coaster when there was no way to escape the wild ride ahead.

She walked directly to a store. It was uncanny how a woman could unerringly locate one particular place in a mall with hundreds of shops. It must be a form of radar.

His mood perked up when he saw where she'd led him. Milady's was a fancy name for an underwear shop, but what they had on display had to be called lingerie. Headless mannequins wearing scraps of cloth presided over racks of tiny panties on hangers, sheer nightgowns and bras that ranged from a couple of inches of satin to engineering marvels.

"What do you need here?" he asked.

"A bra to wear under the dress," she said, searching through a bunch on display.

She picked up a bright red satin one with cups held together by a tiny piece of elastic in front, then a lacy one, also red and so scanty he'd give a week's pay to see Liv wearing it.

She wanted to try them on with the dress, a novel concept to Nick since he couldn't imagine trying on his boxers before he bought them. A young clerk who seemed to be wearing one of the engineered marvels under a tight yellow top pointed Liv toward the dressing room at the back of the store.

Nick watched Liv turn left into a small dressing room where the door was ajar to show it wasn't in use.

This was torture. Behind the flimsy white door, Liv was wasting her nakedness. He could imagine her breasts in one of the red bras. Did she do that peculiar little maneuver women sometimes did, bending forward to fill the cups? Would her nipples be as obvious in the lacy bra as he thought?

Milady's wasn't as busy as most of the mall stores were. Many of the customers wandering around here were men self-consciously shopping for gifts rather than women shopping for themselves. The men were getting the full attention of the clerks.

Nick nonchalantly looked through the arch again. The dressing-room door was shut, but was it locked? As inconspicuously as he could with dozens of bags rustling in his hands, he moved to the door and shifted the sacks to free a couple of fingers. He turned the knob and was delighted when the door eased open.

"Don't scream," he whispered urgently, afraid of startling her. "It's only me." He stepped in and closed the door.

"You aren't supposed to come in here."

"No one saw me. I was careful."

She was stripped to the waist and poised to try on the lacy bra, holding the minuscule bit of lace in front of her.

"You should leave. This isn't the time or the place, and I'm not the woman. Anyway, what if a clerk comes to check?"

He dropped the load of sacks and removed the threat by locking the door.

"They're all too busy helping guys with their Christmas shopping."

She turned her back and leaned forward to let her breasts fall into the cups of the bra. He saw her reflected in the floor-length mirror. The lace didn't conceal her nipples. On the contrary, it created a peekaboo effect that left him a little breathless.

"This would be a good time to see if you have it in you to be spontaneous," he said, hoping he didn't sound as hot and bothered as he felt.

He expected her to have a quiet, ladylike fit since this was Liv. Instead, she turned to face him and eyed the bulge in his jeans.

"You want me to..." She flexed her fingers.

"No. I don't want to be the only one enjoying myself."

He wanted Liv to throw aside her inhibitions and feel something intense. He wanted to shake her composure and make her forget everything but sensation. And he wanted to do it before some nosy clerk came to check.

"Good." She didn't sound like herself, but she didn't shy away. "Let's go for it."

He reached for her and slid her cords down on her thighs, then ran his hands down her back and under the elastic of her pink panties. He loved the smoothness of her skin and the firm roundness of her bottom. Her muscles tightened under his fingers and he gently squeezed.

"I can't believe I'm doing this." She didn't stop him.

He cut off her whisper by gently kissing her, not

wanting to make her walk out of the dressing room with swollen lips. It wasn't his intention to embarrass her, only to demonstrate how much fun it could be to break the rules.

She reached to unzip him and slipped her leg between his. He hadn't expected Liv to take the initiative, but it was incredibly arousing that she did.

He moved his lips to the hollow of her throat, stroking with his tongue as he kneaded the tight flesh of her buttocks. Time stood still, and he had to struggle with himself not to rush her to a climax. It was incredibly important that she be with him all the way, no matter how limited their time was.

"Yes, yes," Liv whispered, running her hands under his shirt and teasing his skin with the feathery rasp of her nails.

He lifted a lace-clad breast in one hand and caressed her hardened nipple with his thumb while he slid the other inside her panties. Her folds were slick with moisture, and she groaned with pleasure. Carefully and slowly, he slid his index finger into the pulsating wetness, at the same time dropping his other hand to tease her from behind.

He ached to be inside her but realized this had to be for Liv. It was his way of telling her that she was incredibly beautiful and sexy.

Their lips were locked together, and the strength

in her arms surprised him as she hugged him tight against her. With more willpower than he knew he possessed, he pushed hard against her pleasure nub, abandoning every thought except giving her a stunning climax.

When she came, she surprised even him, convulsing under his probing hand with an intensity that shook her whole body. She shuddered and came again and again as he urged her on, but she didn't cry out. Her moans were too soft to be heard beyond the walls of the dressing room. When he took his hands away, he kissed her softly, surprisingly satisfied even though there wasn't time for his turn. They'd spent enough time in the dressing room to make the clerk suspicious.

"The lacy bra will do nicely," he said, trying to sound a whole lot calmer than he felt.

He helped her dress in her own clothes, bagged up the red dress she'd left on a corner seat and slipped out ahead of her holding all the shopping bags in front of him. The young clerk in the wired bra gave him an unfriendly look, but he ignored her, opting instead to step out into the mall to wait for Liv.

Through the store entrance he saw Liv buy both bras. Did she want them, or was it a guilt purchase? She came out with her reddish-brown hair firmly tucked behind her ears, the expression on her face knocking him for a loop. Was she mad at him or disappointed in herself?

He knew how much she hated being out of control, and she definitely had been, wildly and erotically so. She'd loved it while it was happening—that he knew for sure—but she wasn't allowing herself to savor the afterglow of a dynamite climax. He pretty much accepted he wasn't going back to her place for anything more.

He braced himself for outrage, indignation or worse. She surprised him.

"Let's have lunch," she said.

She couldn't fool him. She was poised for an explosion, just toying with him before she attacked. He was going to pay for his lesson in spontaneity even though she'd been with him all the way, a willing participant from the word *go*.

"Let's eat at the food court," he suggested. He could play her game, even though he was rock hard and his guts were tied into a roiling mass of knots.

"Sounds okay." She turned in that direction.

At the food court he followed Liv to a Japanese stall and ordered the same meal she did. He couldn't put down the sacks he was holding, so she carried their food to a small round table and went back for soft drinks. He braced himself, anticipating her displeasure.

Nothing happened. They ate lunch, not talking much except to comment on how busy the mall was. Then he drove her home. She didn't invite him to come in. He hadn't really expected it.

Wasn't she going to mention what had happened? He was still shaken by the explosiveness of her climax, but she acted as though nothing had happened. He was never going to understand what made her tick. Maybe no man ever understood a woman, all the more reason not to fall into the delusion that a relationship could last forever.

He had one parting shot when he dropped her off at home.

"I'll see you at your office party. Leave your car home."

"All right." She said it so matter-of-factly she might have been agreeing to take out the trash.

He drove away wondering how he could live for over a week without seeing her again. He'd loved touching her intimately and bringing her to a sensational pleasure peak, but he didn't have a clue how she felt about it.

He didn't even know how he felt.

LIV'S HEAD was in a whirl. As soon as she got home, she tossed her packages and coat on the couch and paced without noticing the wet spots her boots were leaving on the carpet.

She'd never done anything like that before.

No, that just couldn't be. She stopped her frantic pacing and went to the kitchen for a drink of water, then sat down at the kitchen table. Okay, maybe she had been at least a little out of control. She squeezed her thighs together tightly and decided not to kid herself. She'd been way out of control. And it had been *good*.

Was it really so terrible to have sex just for her own pleasure? She'd walked out of the lingerie shop feeling as if she could leap tall buildings.

It would be convenient to blame Nick, but all she'd had to do was say no. And what did he get out of it besides an embarrassing hard-on and the satisfaction of seeing her lose it?

But had she really lost it? A sexy guy had given her a great high as a gift, asking nothing in return. It hadn't been her idea, but she'd certainly been overdue for it. She was young. She was healthy. Her last stab at a relationship had fizzled because Jerry had been a dud. One thing was sure. The next time she had sex, it was going to be her idea. She'd control the pace and pick the place and person. She didn't know whether it would be Nick, but it would be fun.

Right now she needed a distraction. She hung up her coat and found the box of gift wrap on the closet shelf. At least her Christmas shopping was done. Wrapping the gifts would give her something to do. Her mother was easy to please and would love the leather driving gloves and frilly pink housecoat. Dad was harder to buy for, but she'd gone all out with a heather-gray cashmere sweater. Amy had an annoying habit of exchanging gifts, so Liv made sure she kept the sales slip for the beautiful wedding album and gold earrings.

As she wrapped and taped, she couldn't stop thinking about Nick. Should she try to avoid him for the rest of her life? She wasn't sure how, since he'd appointed himself her date for the office party. Could former lovers enjoy a casual but fun-filled relationship without emotional entanglements? Nick could, but could she? Should she try with him? Would she have the opportunity? This line of thought was a little scary, but it was hard to put what had happened out of her mind.

When all her gifts were wrapped, there were still two sacks lying on the couch. She took out the red dress and held it against her. It looked even better than she remembered, with long, tight-fitting sleeves, a revealing scoop neckline and a skirt that swirled at midthigh.

Red wasn't usually her color, but she hadn't been able to resist. It was a dress designed for fun, but it wouldn't hurt to show her boss she knew how to lighten up.

She dumped the two red bras out of the sack from Milady's. She didn't even know if either would look good under the dress. She'd been in shock when she bought them, not quite believing what she'd let happen in the dressing room.

She stood dangling the bras and tormenting her conscience, then gradually found a reason to smile. Nick had rocked her world, but he didn't have to know it.

He'd been baffled by what he saw as her matter-of-fact reaction. She should get an Academy Award for her performance at lunch. She'd done her absolute best to act as though nothing important had happened. Even though it had. It had cost her dearly during their lunch. Her bowl of rice and stir-fry vegetables had had all the appeal of sawdust, and her stomach was still in knots. But she hadn't made any recriminations or, worse still, given the least hint that the experience had rocked her world.

She started pacing again. How was she going to get Nick out of her system once and for all? He could turn her on with a glance. His intimate touch made her crazy. Her college affair with him had been a brushfire compared to the firestorm raging in her now.

She was hooked again, but there had to be a way to get him out of her system. She didn't want to be dumped again. It was time she took control of her love life the way she did everything else that concerned her.

She ran upstairs to her office, found a new yellow pad and grabbed a trusty ballpoint.

"Number one," she said, sitting down to write. "Refuse to see Nick ever again."

No, that wouldn't work. If Nick wanted to see her, he'd track her all the way to Bora-Bora. She ripped off that page and started another. She wrote: Talk marriage.

That would scare him off for sure, but getting hitched didn't have anything to do with the way she felt now. Partly because of her parents' divorce, but mainly because of who she was now, she wasn't willing to take a chance on someone like Nick. She needed to get him out of her system so she wouldn't be tempted to make the mistake of relying on him a second time. The question was how? She tore off another page and tossed it in the general direction of her wastebasket.

"Think," she urged herself.

Suddenly the solution was obvious. She wrote in

big black letters: Show Nick she was a different person now.

He'd originally been attracted to her when she was sweet and restrained. Maybe if he saw the new Liv of today, he'd fade out of her life. She was scared of what she was starting to feel for him again, but no way would she let him start up with her, then drop her when he felt like it. This time she was in control, and the office party was just the place to demonstrate it.

10

HERE SHE WAS having two dates in one weekend, Liv wryly thought as she dressed in black pants and a white shirt. Her social life needed a transfusion when she started counting dinner with her father as a date.

She put on her coat just before he was due at six. Predictably, Dad rang her buzzer exactly on the hour. Nick had been right about one thing. She did get her passion for organization from her father.

Did her parents' marriage go sour because Mom got tired of being micromanaged? Or did Dad's frustration become unbearable after nearly thirty years of his wife's scatterbrained ways? It was also possible they had other problems that they concealed from their children, but Liv wasn't sure she wanted to know. She didn't want to take sides or assign blame. She felt protective toward her mother, but she still needed Dad's strength and reliability.

She opened the door and hugged him.

"Liv, honey, I've missed you." He stepped back and smiled warmly.

"You could've called." She couldn't help reproaching him for his silence.

"I could blame the flu. I was laid low for a couple of days, but mostly I didn't know what to say to you. Amy is taking the divorce hard, but I know you'll be able to deal with it."

"You don't need to be concerned about me." She didn't want to have this conversation. That's why she had her coat on, ready to go.

"It's a father's prerogative to worry," he said.

Liv pulled on her gloves so she wouldn't have to look directly at her father. In his early fifties, Doug Kearns was a handsome man, with dark eyes that Liv had inherited. His black hair was turning silvery in an attractive way, softening his somewhat sharp nose and jaw. This evening he was dressed casually, which was unusual for him. A burgundy sweater showed between the lapels of his overcoat.

Naturally slender, he looked a little gaunt to Liv. She didn't have trouble believing he'd had the flu, not that Dad ever tried to deceive her.

"I thought we'd go to Jed's Pancake House," he said.

He would suggest the restaurant she'd loved as a child. She wasn't in the mood for a nostalgic supper, but he'd be disappointed if she suggested another place.

He drove and parked in a half-full parking lot beside a white block building with a royal-blue roof. The place appeared shabbier than she remembered it, especially inside where the blue leather seats in the booths were looking worn.

She ordered pancakes with a maple-pecan topping. Dad had the same platter of buckwheats with bacon he'd ordered for as long as she could remember.

They talked about her job, the weather, his business, the slow service in the restaurant and the mediocre pancakes they finally got. When Dad pushed aside his platter of half-eaten buckwheats, Liv knew he was ready to say whatever was really on his mind.

"I talked to your mother yesterday," he said. "Seems she's going to Milwaukee for Christmas."

"I knew Sean's parents had invited her. She's decided for sure to go?"

Liv wondered why she was out of the loop when it came to her parents' plans. Did they expect her to disapprove of everything they did? Was Nick right in thinking she tried to control too many things?

"Yes, she's going, so that leaves you and me for the holidays. The trouble is, your grandparents are very upset about the divorce. I thought I should fly down to Florida over Christmas. I had my secretary check flights, and she just got me a single seat for Orlando on the twenty-second. If you want to come with me, I'll try rebooking for another day. Maybe we can get something on Christmas Day. I'm taking some time off, so I won't be coming back until New Year's Day."

"Orlando would be great." She sighed.

She imagined walking on a sandy beach with sunny skies and no worries. Her grandmother would make turkey with walnut dressing and pumpkin pie with loads of whipped topping. Granddad would challenge her to an endless game of gin rummy and regale her with hilarious stories. What could be nicer than spending Christmas with grandparents who loved to pamper and spoil her?

"But I can't," she said forlornly. "I have so much to do at work, I don't have time to take any vacation."

She didn't want to burden her father with worries about job insecurity. He had enough problems of his own at the moment.

"I guess you don't want to miss the office Christmas party," her father teased.

She wouldn't mind passing it up for a chance to see her grandparents, but Billy was big on group gatherings that included spouses, significant others, girlfriends and, of course, boyfriends. Nick would come in handy, just so long as she kept her head. Maybe she should just skip the party altogether.

"I sure hate leaving you here alone on Christmas," her father said.

"Don't worry, Dad. I'll be fine."

"I thought the three of us—you, me and Amy—could get together next Sunday. You know, exchange presents and toast the New Year too."

"That would be nice, Dad."

"Good, I'll set it up with Amy and let you know. And I'll call you from Florida on Christmas Day. You can explain to your grandparents that it's not my fault you stayed in Chicago." He smiled to show he didn't blame her.

Dad drove her home and stayed a short while, but declined an offer to stay with her until he made arrangements for an apartment. Even after he left for his motel, she couldn't quite believe her family would be apart at Christmas. Fortunately, she had too much work to dwell on the thought.

Nick didn't call Sunday or Monday. Apparently he'd been sincere about not needing more help with the Merris story. It wasn't like Nick to quit. Maybe that came from being an only child. He'd grown up thinking all things were possible and rarely gave up on anything—except their relationship.

She was much better off without him. Old feelings

were creeping back. She found herself thinking about him far too much, but one thing was sure. Nick still wanted a life unencumbered by commitments.

When she got to work Tuesday morning, she had so much to do she actually welcomed help from her intern. She sent Brandi Jo to do some research as soon as she got to the office, a useful way to keep her out of Liv's space.

Liv went back to the presentation she was preparing, hoping it was good enough to snare some new clients and save her job. But she was glad when Dana came into her office to touch base.

"Am I interrupting?" her petite, black-haired friend asked.

"Yes, but come in anyway and sit down. I'm hoping all our clients will go somewhere for the holidays and give me a chance to catch up. What's up with you?"

Dana smiled slyly. "New man on the scene. Unfortunately he can't come to the Christmas party. I wanted to show him off. He does have a friend who—"

"No, no! No blind dates for me. Actually I'm going to the party with Nick Matheson. Remember, I've told you about him."

"Not *the* Nick?"

"Yes, but it's no big deal. We're just old friends. You know the routine."

"You slept with him for a year, and now you're good friends?" Dana gave Liv a deeply skeptical look.

"Nowhere near a year. Anyway, why can't a man and a woman be friends?"

Dana was only saying what Liv had wondered herself, but the subject was too complicated to talk about when they both should be working. Dana left to keep an appointment, but Liv couldn't turn off her thoughts about Nick long enough to get much done.

She shook her head to erase memories of their day at the mall. What they'd shared probably didn't mean nearly as much to Nick as it did to her. Maybe she'd made too much of their short relationship herself. He'd always been friendly and demonstrative, probably because his parents were that way. Once, she'd gone to his mother's for dinner before she moved away. It had been hugs all around. His father sold farm equipment, apparently with quite a bit of success, and he radiated the easy friendliness of a gifted salesman.

She couldn't believe Nick wasn't going to ask her for more help with Matilda Merris. Was it possible he wasn't pressuring her because he felt a little guilty for what had happened five years ago? Was he trying to make up for it? He'd certainly been sympathetic about her parents.

She didn't want comforting from Nick. Neither did she require any more help from him in being spontaneous, but she could try to live up to her end of the bargain. She'd try Matilda once more, this time using all the skills she'd learned in the public relations profession.

She reached the artist on her first try.

"Miss Merris, this is Olivia Kearns at William Lawrence Associates. I really hate bothering you again, but I understand you're quite active in artistic circles. You probably know Chicago's museums well, but it occurred to me that you may not know about Chicago's newest one."

Liv had said the magic words: art and museum. Artists lived to have work exhibited in a prestigious institution. For the next fifteen minutes Liv talked art with the woman and explained the plan for the new sports museum.

"I can't believe someone collected memorabilia about my father," Matilda said thoughtfully.

"So you see," Liv said, "Nick Matheson doesn't want to cause you any pain. He genuinely wants your father to have a positive place in Chicago sports history."

"I don't know if I'm up to talking about the scandal," Matilda said sadly.

"I don't want to rush you into something distressing," Liv said. "Why don't you think about it for a few days. There's a collector who very much wants to honor your father's exceptional talent."

"I'll give it some thought," the elderly woman said. "But please don't call me again until after Christmas. It's a busy time of year, so I won't be much help to you."

"I promise not to rush you," Liv said, ending the conversation with a cheerful, "Merry Christmas."

She'd done it! Her public relations skills were still razor sharp, especially when Nick wasn't in the room distracting her. Matilda could still say no, but Liv was hopeful. Best of all, she'd been truthful and sincere in presenting her case—Nick's case.

There was plenty of room in the PR business for her talent and ability. Let the Brandi Jo's of the world flaunt their sexuality. Liv would keep on doing what she did best. If Billy didn't appreciate her, someone else would. Of course, she'd prefer to keep the job she had, but that was a problem she'd worry about later.

She was eager to tell Nick. She called the *Chicago Post*, only to be told he was out, but she was able to send an e-mail message. She checked at half-hour intervals the rest of the day, but when she left for home, he hadn't yet responded.

She checked her home computer as soon as she got home and found a message from Nick waiting for her:

Good girl! I'll drop by later for details. Nick

What was this "good girl" stuff? He made it sound as if Santa would put something especially nice in her stocking. She sat for a few minutes before deleting his message.

Was she ready to report to Nick face-to-face? E-mails were much safer, but he'd undoubtedly show up if there was a chance his story was back on track. If he turned on the charm again, how would she handle it?

She hated feeling ambiguous but she didn't want to put Nick completely out of her life just yet. She wanted him as a friend on her own terms.

Maybe the best defense was a good offense. She didn't usually think in combative terms, but this was Nick she was trying to resist.

She had it right about Nick's interest in Matilda. Her phone rang. He wanted to come over and talk about Matilda on his way home. She'd expected him to contact her and wanted to see him again, but part of her doubted the wisdom of it. Before he got there, she changed out of her wool skirt. The white semi-sheer blouse she was wearing would do, especially after she opened the top three buttons to reveal cleavage between the cups of her lacy bra. Jeans didn't cut it for a femme fatale, so she rummaged in her closet and found a pair of black cropped pants Amy had given her when she got tired of them. Liv had never worn them, but she was a saver. There was always a possibility her sister would want them back, and Liv had a whole garment bag full of Amy's castoffs.

"Matheson, eat your heart out," she said, slipping into mules and checking out her backside in the mirror. She could be as naughty as the next girl, and tonight she was going to enjoy herself.

She'd kept her part of the bargain by calling Matilda again. Now she had to prove to herself she could be with Nick without getting emotionally involved. It was about feeling good about herself, not about falling in love. What woman wouldn't enjoy having a great-looking guy hanging around? In fact, she felt like making her place a little more romantic.

She put out all the candles she had and turned down the lights, then fluffed pillows on the couch and surveyed her work.

Nick tended to run late, so the buzzer startled her

when it rang sooner than she'd expected. She peeked out her spy hole and saw Nick standing in the yellowish light, his head bare and his coat open even though the temperature had dropped to near zero. He had the sweet expression of a little boy.

She opened the door, and all illusion of boyishness disappeared from his face. He stepped inside, closed the door and handed her a dark green bottle with a foil-covered cork.

"Champagne," he said, grinning. "To celebrate. I came as soon as I could."

"You can't be late since you didn't mention when you'd get here." The champagne was cold, and she held it away from her while he took off his coat and boots.

"Let me open this, then you can tell me about Matilda." He led the way to the kitchen.

"It's not news that calls for champagne," she said. His eyes lingered on her cleavage, and Liv knew he wasn't as cool as he pretended to be. The important thing was that she could enjoy his company but end their time together whenever she liked. She wasn't under his spell the way she once had been.

He opened a cupboard but didn't take out any of her water or juice glasses.

"You must have wineglasses," he said.

"The shelf above the fridge."

Champagne was a better idea than she'd first thought. The stuff went to her head, but she didn't care whether she got a little silly tonight.

"I guess you're here to talk about Matilda," she said as he poured for both of them.

"Did you wear that outfit to talk about a dead baseball player?" He gave her a searching look with his sexy eyes.

"Why not?" she said.

He raised one eyebrow, then handed her a goblet filled nearly to the brim with bubbly.

"Let's sit down," he said.

"I don't have all that much to report," she said, following him to the living room. "I explained to her about the sports museum."

"Did you mention my editor's collection?" He was standing near the opposite end of the coffee table from her.

"Yes, but I didn't say who owned it, only that a collector was willing to donate it if the museum would accept."

"Perfect."

"Matilda hasn't agreed to talk to you yet. She wants time to think about it, but she did sound interested."

"Not so good." He took a big swallow of champagne. "When will she decide?"

"After Christmas. That's the best I could do," she said defensively.

"You've more than kept your part of the bargain. It's a whole lot more than I was able to do." He lowered his voice to the seductive tone that used to drive her to distraction.

He walked to her end of the table and held out his half-empty glass.

"To you, for doing more than I had any right to ask. You are one special lady, Olivia Kearns, and I intend to make sure your boss appreciates you more."

"You really don't need to. I wasn't that serious about our bargain."

Even in the light of a single floor lamp, she could see he'd recently shaved. She noted the faint spiciness of his cologne. He wore a white shirt underneath a navy blue sweater. She noticed his charcoal wool trousers, and wondered if he'd dressed up for her.

"You're more than halfway there. You look spectacular tonight."

She'd expected him to mention it, but his voice was so soft and sexy it made her shiver.

He picked up the bottle and took the goblet from her, wrapping a towel around the bottle to catch drops as he refilled the glass.

"It's good." Could she have come up with something more inane to say?

He reached out with one finger and ran it across her lips.

Her blood was boiling. She wanted Nick to get hot and bothered, but she was squirming inside. And he hadn't even kissed her yet.

He took the champagne away from her about two nanoseconds before she was going to drop it and put both goblets on the table.

"Saturday was the nicest day I've had in a long time," he said quietly, circling her mouth with the tip of his finger.

"We did a lot of shopping."

"And more."

He was good at seductive small talk, but she wanted to be the one to seduce him if anything was going to happen.

"Thank you," he whispered close to her ear.

"It was only a phone call." His lips brushed her forehead, and she closed her eyes, trying to forget how gorgeous he was.

"I meant, thank you for wearing these." He slid his hands down her sides then cupped her buttocks and pressed closer.

He covered her mouth with a slow, hard kiss that

took away her breath. His hands continued to caress her, and she felt like melting.

She tried to say, "Stop," then remembered she didn't want him to. Every fiber in her body responded when he parted her lips and found the soft crevasses of her mouth with his tongue.

She hardly noticed when he slipped open the glass buttons on her blouse and slid it down her shoulders. Cool air wafted over her torso, and Nick bent his head to nuzzle the hollow between her breasts. She was pretty sure she'd die if he stopped, and she clutched the sleeves of his sweater to steady herself.

"I love the taste of your skin," he whispered.

He slid his hands down her body to her thighs, driving her closer to the edge. Now was the time to push him away. She didn't want to be a tease, and she could feel herself weakening. Not even Nick could expect to have sex whenever he wanted to with the woman he'd dumped.

She should call a halt, but Nick's lips tempted her to override her better judgment.

He began lowering her zipper, but she was still in control. She really was. She could stop him anytime, but it felt so good to be touched by Nick. He had magic hands. She closed her eyes to savor the moment.

"I knew you weren't wearing panties," he whispered wickedly, inching one finger below the zipper and making her gasp.

"This isn't a good idea." She told herself she meant it, but she was liquefying under his touch.

"Please, baby, I'm past the point of no return."

She'd never heard him beg. Ignoring her own good sense, she reached out and found his erection straining against the smooth wool of his pants. She didn't plan to torture him just to assert control in the situation, but she couldn't resist pressing hard against him as he lowered his mouth to hers for a long, deep kiss. She pushed his hand away and took the initiative, quickly zipping his pants open. She couldn't do less for him than he'd done for her.

He was wearing black cotton briefs stretched to the max to contain him.

"Liv, sweetheart..."

Whatever he intended to say, she didn't need to hear it. She rolled his briefs down on his thighs and reached for him with both hands. Friends did favors for friends. She was only paying him back for the dressing room because it had been exciting for her. She still felt in control. She wasn't being swept off her feet.

"Let me," he began, but again she cut him off, this time by squeezing him with gentle pressure, then rolling his penis between her palms. She remembered how beautiful Nick was. He was hugely magnificent when he was fully aroused. It was the biggest mystery about men. How could something so hard feel so velvety soft to the touch? "Let me love you all the way," he murmured.

He halfheartedly attempted to move her hands off, but this had nothing to do with love and everything to do with being in control of her own desires. She wasn't going to stop now.

She did what he'd taught her years ago, not stopping until he groaned with release.

"Let's go up to your bedroom," he rasped.

He kissed her eyelids and ran his lips down her cheek until their mouths connected.

"You're beautiful," he murmured. "Beautiful, sexy and smart. I must've been crazy to leave you."

She should send him away now just to prove that she could, but it felt wonderful to be in the circle of his arms, her leg captured between his thighs.

"We're only friends now." She said it aloud but was talking to herself.

"Friends who help each other. There's so much I'd like to teach you."

He scooped her into his arms and carried her up the stairs. She should protest, but if she was a willing participant, her eyes not clouded by infatuation or love, was she any less her own person? She decided not.

"Which room?" he asked.

"There." She pointed.

When he placed her on the comforter that covered her bed, she admitted to herself that she'd wanted this since he first came to her office.

11

NICK DIDN'T KNOW what he was doing. Should he really be here with Liv? He'd hurried to her house because he was excited about the Merris story. Just when he'd almost given up like the other reporters who'd tried, he had another shot at talking to Matilda, thanks to Liv.

The champagne had probably been a bad idea, but neither of them was tipsy, only loose and uninhibited, the things she'd wanted him to teach her.

He wanted her naked, and with Liv helping him he quickly undressed her. He then stood to strip off his own clothes, his breath coming in raw gasps. At least since meeting Liv again, he was always, optimistically, prepared.

"Liv, sweetheart," he whispered, returning to her and enveloping her in his arms.

He held her against his length, her flesh warm and firm against him.

"This is just for fun," she whispered, making him pause for a moment.

"Of course it's fun. How could it not be?"

"I mean, it doesn't mean anything else. We're not back together. It's no big deal, just two friends getting together."

She was offering him a dream scenario, sex with no ties or obligations. He should be happier than he was, but her words cooled him down—at least for a minute or so.

He didn't know how to answer, but he did know how to please her. He kissed her slowly, gradually parting her lips and thrusting his tongue deeply into her mouth. She responded with all the fervor any man could expect, kissing his face and chest until he was ready to explode.

When he straddled her legs, he was as bemused as he was aroused. Shy, reserved Olivia had always had a wild side when she allowed herself to let loose. It had been beyond his hopes that it would happen again with him. She embraced him with her legs and pulled him down until he was deep inside of her, moving in concert until he went a little crazy.

She came before him and cried out again and again, staying with him until his control shattered and they collapsed together. Even then he didn't stop kissing her face and body, loving the sheen of her skin and its sweet fragrance. He pulled her into his arms, stroking her hair and wanting to prolong the moment. When she fell asleep, he was content to keep her nestled against his chest.

He woke up to find the light still on and Liv quietly sleeping in the crook of his arm. Big green numbers on her bedside clock showed it was past midnight, but he didn't have the willpower to get up and go home. He scooped her even closer and was pleased when her eyelids fluttered and opened. He'd told her she was beautiful, but it had been an understatement. Her features were stunning. He'd never seen more adorable lips, pink and full over bright white teeth. She smiled easily, laughed prettily and kissed with gusto.

She liked the same movies and music he did, was quick to pick up on a joke and was kind and considerate. Added to all that, she rocked in bed. She knew how to turn him on and inside out. She made him feel seven feet tall and sexier than any guy had a right to feel.

He'd come to her house hoping to make love to her, but what had happened exceeded his expectations.

She stirred against his side, and he reached over to cup one breast, marveling at the rosy-brown perfection of her nipple.

He wanted Liv to wake up for more torrid sex, but what about tomorrow and the next day and next year? Was he going to be able to let her go again? Did he want to? What was this new obsession he had with her? How long would it take to satisfy his longing for her, if it could be done? His aversion to commitment hadn't changed, but Liv had.

And what the hell was this "no big deal, just friends" stuff? Was she purposely trying to be less inhibited and more spontaneous? He'd had glimpses before of just how passionate she could be, but he also knew she fought against this side of her nature. How much had she changed since they'd been together five years ago? He was puzzled but intrigued.

It was close to noon before Nick could rouse himself to leave, and go to work. Even then he couldn't get Liv out of his mind. Maybe the champagne had been the cause of her exuberance, but he didn't remember her drinking that much bubbly. What he did remember was mostly X-rated.

He arrived back at the office with little interest in working.

"Do you still want the Tuesday before Christmas off?" Kurt asked, stopping by his desk. "I found out I can cover for you."

"Do I ever! Thanks a lot!"

He would be seeing Liv again at her office party, and he had a few days to figure out what to say. He hadn't been using his brain when he'd let things escalate between them. Grateful as he was to have another shot at the Merris story, it wasn't important compared to figuring out where he and Liv stood. Just friends? That seemed unlikely. What he was feeling for Liv was much more serious.

The more he thought, the more morose he felt. Their time together in grad school had been terrific, but the timing had been really bad. He was just getting over the shock of learning his parents had stayed together mostly for his sake. He'd gradually deduced that Dad had had a series of affairs. Nick didn't want a relationship based on deceit, but was he any more capable of staying faithful to one woman than his father had been?

He didn't want to hurt Liv again, but he didn't know how to fit her into his life.

He was still light-years way from wanting a permanent relationship. He wasn't going to make the same mistake his father had, but Liv deserved to know where they stood. He'd never met a woman like her. Sometimes she was a control freak, but peel away the layers of her personality and she could be a wild woman. Just when he thought she wasn't spontaneous or adventurous, she pulled a surprise like last night. Would he ever understand her? Could he ever do without her again? He didn't have a clue what to do. He didn't even know what he wanted, let alone what was on her mind.

"Hello?" Kurt asked, because Nick hadn't taken in a word he'd been saying.

"Sorry, things on my mind." Why was he doing this to himself? He had to snap out of it. "Chinese buffet okay with you for lunch? My treat."

Liv deserved better than he was ready to offer, but strangely, she hadn't shown the slightest interest in anything more than hot sex.

He didn't have more time to dwell on Liv. Mack wanted a progress report on the Merris story, and finally Nick had something positive to tell him.

FRIDAY MORNING Liv was looking forward to Brandi Jo's farewell luncheon with a decided lack of enthusiasm.

Dana had saved the day. Her aunt's cousin was a world-class Italian cook who could sometimes be persuaded to prepare a meal for groups under fifty. The important thing was not to be upstaged by Brandi Jo. Liv dug into her sister's castoffs at the back of her closet and came up with a pale blue wraparound dress that felt like a second skin. It wasn't her, but it was hot compared to her usual office wear.

She'd tried hard to put Nick out of her mind, but it

was nearly impossible not to remember the way his face had softened with passion. When he was aroused, his eyes looked cloudy under hooded lids. It was a look she'd carry with her as long as she lived, but for her own protection, she hoped never to see it again. It would be so much better for her if she never saw him again, but when someone knocked softly on her office door, she instinctively hoped it was Nick on the other side.

The door opened partway, and Dana stuck her head through the opening.

"Oh, it's you," Liv said, relieved and disappointed at the same time.

"I just wanted you to know Mrs. Rico will be here in plenty of time to set up for noon," Dana said. "I checked with her last night."

"You're a lifesaver!"

Liv felt like hugging her friend, but what she did instead was compliment her on her lively outfit. Dana's short floral skirt and coral sweater wouldn't be upstaged by anything in Brandi Jo's juvenile wardrobe.

Both of them went back to work, but Brandi Jo's hour came all too soon. Most of the office staff came in one wave, but Brandi Jo made a late entrance to be sure she was the center of attention. Dressed in a purple miniskirt and white angora sweater that plunged nearly to her navel, she did know how to get attention. Billy Lawrence hovered over her throughout the luncheon, but he did make it a point to congratulate Liv on putting the event together on short notice. Liv tried to give the credit to Dana, but her boss wasn't big on listening.

Liv went back to her office with a severe case of Friday-afternoon blahs. She wanted to brood in silent solitude, but Boz burst into the room with his usual bustle.

"Great buffet, Liv. Nice outfit too. Glad to see you're on board with the right image for William Lawrence Associates."

"Thank you."

"I didn't have a chance to talk to you this morning," Boz said, "but I have a lead on a potential client named J. B. Davenport who could turn your career around. A consortium wants to open a chain of sports bars in the city and suburbs. We have a good shot at handling their PR. They'll need some celebrities at the openings plus an ongoing campaign. I'm tossing the presentation your way. I can't emphasize too much how important it is to the firm and to Billy to get more clients like this."

"I'll do my best," she said, mustering as much enthusiasm as she could.

Boz was offering her a job saver, but she didn't kid

herself. Who else would slave over the holidays on a presentation that might not pan out? Someone with no life, that's who.

After Boz left, she had a visitor. Although part of her knew this wasn't the time or place to see Nick again, she was happy to see him.

"Hi. Hope I'm not interrupting anything. I just happened to be in the neighborhood," he said without his usual cocky grin.

He was standing stiffly just inside the door. Was it possible he felt awkward?

"Hi. Did you want to talk about Matilda?" Somehow they hadn't gotten around to it last night.

"No, I understand I can't contact her until after Christmas. I wondered if you're free for dinner tonight."

"I'm not sure that's a good idea."

"We need to talk about last night."

She shook her head. What possible good could come of it? She couldn't let Nick become an important part of her life. She was as determined as ever not to let herself fall in love with him again.

"We still have to work on your new image—for your job. I got a few ideas from our fashion editor. She's big on makeovers."

"Thanks, but not tonight, okay?"

Before she could give him a reason, he took her in

his arms and kissed her so hard it knocked the breath out of her, then he kissed her again even though she was too conscious of being in her office to respond.

"It would be a quickie—dinner, that is. I have a hockey game to cover tonight."

She loved his kisses but didn't want him to know how badly she wanted them to go on and on. She couldn't risk another heartbreaking disappointment.

"We had a going-away luncheon for my intern. I'm too stuffed to even think of dinner. Anyway, I need to get home early tonight. I have lots to do."

"I'll see you at your Christmas party then," he said cheerfully on his way out. "Take care."

Look at the good side, she told herself. At least she'd have a date—and she was sure to see Nick one more time.

SUNDAY SHE RUSHED through the supermarket and got what she needed for her family's traditional Christmas dinner. While she cooked for Amy and her dad, she tried to fool herself into thinking she was only seeing Nick again for kicks. Her meal preparations were much more successful than this delusion. She felt hollow inside because she didn't know what she wanted. She'd slept with Nick because she wanted to feel in control of her life. She wanted to be the one to call the shots when they were together. In college she'd never made a deliberate decision to have sex with him. She'd just been so crazy in love that anything he wanted seemed wonderful. Now she had doubts about everything she'd done, past and present. Was she capable of being cool and levelheaded where Nick was concerned? Was she leaving herself wide open for more pain and rejection?

Dad arrived first for the family party. Amy came by herself twenty minutes later.

"Isn't Sean coming?" Liv asked as her sister took off her coat.

"No, I'll talk to you later about him," Amy whispered, handing her coat to Liv and moving to the couch where Dad was checking out the news on TV. "Hey, where's your tree? Your place doesn't look at all like Christmas."

"I didn't have time to decorate."

All three of them tried to pretend they were one happy family celebrating Christmas. Mom had refused to join them, saying it would be too awkward for her to spend it with Dad.

They ate a big turkey dinner with stuffing and sweet potatoes, then opened gifts. Her father got Liv a new printer that she badly needed, three sweaters, because he couldn't decide on a color, and a birthstone locket. He was especially generous with his daughters, giving Amy a DVD player, two blouses and a pair of earrings.

Liv hugged her father and thanked him again for the gifts when he was ready to leave. Amy hovered. She had something on her mind.

"I'm not sure about anything anymore," Amy said when they were alone. "I'm not even sure I want a wedding."

"You're the only one who can decide that," Liv said sympathetically. "If you have serious doubts..."

"Sean couldn't even be bothered to come here tonight. He made up an excuse about flying to Minneapolis this evening so he could keep an appointment in the morning."

"Maybe his boss insisted he go," Liv suggested mildly.

"Oh, probably, but that's not the point. He was glad he had an excuse not to come with me tonight."

"Maybe he felt awkward. Without Mom, it wasn't our usual family holiday."

"It wasn't about her. He should've wanted to be here for my sake." Amy sounded on the verge of tears.

"Maybe you're more upset about the divorce than you realize. If you want to postpone your wedding..."

"We can't postpone it! We booked the church and the reception hall. My bridesmaids have paid for their dresses. The tux rental alone costs an arm and a leg, and they don't return deposits. We can't put it off. Dad would lose thousands of dollars, and he wouldn't even get a son-in-law. He likes Sean."

"What can I say?" Liv felt truly helpless. Usually Amy's problems were relatively easy to solve. "You do love Sean, don't you?"

"Yes. Well, I think I do, but how can anyone be sure it's the real thing?"

Liv shook her head, at a loss for what to say. Love was so dynamic and special it couldn't be defined with words. It was the way her whole day brightened when she saw Nick. She'd rather be with him than anyone in the world. But love could be painful too, the gut-wrenching agony of knowing you shouldn't be with the only person you wanted. Was she falling in love with him again? It certainly felt that way to her.

"Don't throw away the relationship until you're absolutely sure," Liv said softly. "That's all I can say. You have to work it out with Sean."

"You're right as usual." Amy sounded even more morose. "I've got to stop coming to you with my problems."

"You're my sister. I love you. You can come to me anytime, but I don't have all the answers."

"I'm curious," Amy said. "Did my matchmaking get any results? Have you seen Nick?"

"Actually I have. We went shopping last weekend. And he came here one evening."

"That makes it sound like you're dating again." Amy sounded excited. "Are you going to get back together?"

"This time it's only for fun," she said, as eager to convince herself as Amy. "Neither of us is involved with anyone else right now so... We're just friends—casual friends."

"You're the world's worst liar," Amy said. "You've slept with him."

"Only once. It didn't mean anything."

Amy looked skeptical but didn't say anything.

"It seemed like a good idea at the time. That doesn't mean we're involved again. There's absolutely nothing wrong with having a little fun. Knowing him before just made it easier, more convenient." She was talking too much. Amy looked even more dubious.

"Convenient sex with Nick Matheson." Amy grinned. "I'd sooner believe the Cubs will win three World Series in a row. You're never casual about anything."

Busted by her own sister!

"Things have a way of working out," Amy said, exactly what Liv had intended to say to her.

When Amy left, Liv wondered if she'd ever know for sure what she really wanted from life.

12

MOST OF BILLY LAWRENCE'S employees decided the day of the office Christmas party was a day to not work. The employees' lounge was crowded in the morning, and clumps of mistletoe were dangling in the most unlikely places. When she got her coffee, Liv felt as if she was the only one working.

She was too concerned about her sports-bar presentation to blow off work. Even though people kept popping into her office, regaling her with corny jokes and urging her to join them, she continued working.

Before she could feel confident about approaching a potential client, she had to do background research. When she went to the meeting, she'd know all there was to know about the people involved and sports bars in general.

She could work through noise, interruptions and clumsy attempts to lure her under the mistletoe, but her concentration was poor when she thought of Nick. He hadn't called, so she didn't know whether he'd actually show up for the party. Maybe he was having second thoughts about getting close to her again.

She was still hard at work when Nick showed up at four-thirty looking especially handsome with a new haircut, a navy suit and a pale blue shirt with a red paisley tie.

"Ready to party?" he asked.

"Not quite. I have to finish printing out some research. Why don't you join the party, and I'll be done soon."

"I don't mind waiting here." He sat and crossed one leg over his knee.

"I'll get it done faster if you leave."

"How long will it take you?"

"Half an hour, tops. There's food in the conference room. Why don't you go help yourself."

"Okay, I am hungry. No time for lunch. But I'll only go if you promise to lose the sweater."

"I'll leave it in the office when I join you."

"Do it now. I want to see you."

He walked over to her, sliding the white sweater away from her shoulders and kissing the side of her neck.

"You look gorgeous. I'm tempted to give you a hickey," he said, nuzzling her throat.

"Just go!" she said affectionately.

"I'm off to the buffet table." He threw her off balance by teasing her ear with his tongue. "If you're not out in thirty minutes, I'll sling you over my shoulder and carry you to the party."

She got shivers down her spine from Nick's teasing threat. He left but she couldn't work anymore. She waited fifteen long, agonizing minutes so he wouldn't think she'd been lying about having work, then patted her hair, adjusted the sexy but not particularly comfortable bra, and sallied forth to find her man—she meant her date.

She checked first in the conference room where food was spread out. Billy had gone all out for the party, hiring professional decorators to turn the place into a winter wonderland. Several artificial Christmas trees sparkled with fake snow and silver and blue balls. People surrounded a buffet table spread out with the usual finger foods plus sandwich loaves cut into tree and bell shapes and frosted with cream cheese. The staff had already helped themselves liberally to the smoked oysters, shrimp and salmon, but Nick was nowhere to be seen.

NICK HAD IMPATIENTLY snacked on a few appetizers, but he was hungry for Liv, not food. He circulated through the spacious suite of rooms, killing time and resisting the urge to go back to her office and hurry her along.

Then he spotted her ahead of him, alone on the other side of the bottled-drinking-water stand with her back turned and no one else in the immediate area.

He came up behind her, slipped his arms around her waist and nuzzled the back of her neck without letting her see him.

"Mmm. Did you bring mistletoe?" she whispered.

He didn't answer. He discreetly moved one hand to her breast, ready to duck if she hauled off and socked him. Instead, she moaned and covered his hand with hers, then tilted her face to his.

Just how long did they have to stay at the party? He wanted to be alone with Liv, the sooner the better. "Is there anyplace we can be alone?" he whispered.

"I guess if a couple was really determined, they could find some little nook for a private conversation."

"It's your turf," he said. "Lead the way."

He was incredibly turned on by Liv's compliance. Was she really going to go along with what he had in mind? Maybe she was only toying with him.

"First we have to be seen," she said.

He groaned but knew she was right. He'd have to glad-hand her boss before she felt comfortable sneaking away.

They circulated for what seemed like hours, but it was only half an hour. He met Billy Lawrence, found out his sport was horse racing and met someone called Bosworth who wanted to talk about the Super Bowl. He was used to sports fans bending his ear when they heard he worked for the *Post*, but he had other things in mind tonight. He predicted Bosworth's team would bomb, which effectively cut off that conversation.

"When?" he whispered impatiently to Liv.

"It's really warm in here," she said in a louder-than-necessary voice. "Let's go out in the corridor and cool off."

"Good idea." He put his hand on her waist and guided her to the door. A short way down the corridor one of the three elevator doors opened and a couple got off.

"This way," Liv said, grabbing his hand and racing to stop the elevator from shutting them out.

"There won't be anyone on the fourteenth floor," she said, pushing the button. "One suite isn't occupied, and a group of orthodontists have the rest of the floor. They'll be gone by now."

He watched the numbers above the door until the elevator stopped at fourteen.

"Take off your shoe," she said. "My heels are too flimsy."

He knew she wanted to keep the door from closing all the way so the elevator couldn't move. The evening had gotten much more interesting.

"I'm getting too old to play games," she said as he took her in his arms. "I've tried every way I know to get you out of my system—every way but one."

"What's that?" He was having difficulty breathing.

"We'll have to get tired of each other."

He couldn't imagine ever getting tired of her, but hot sex might save his sanity and keep him from making a big mistake like tying himself down for life. He was awestruck that she was letting her wild side take over, if only for this moment in time.

"Let's go to your place," he said.

"No."

"My place?" He was suspicious, but Liv would never suggest anything as wild as what he had in mind. "I want to spend the night with you."

"Okay, but first..."

"What are you doing?" He knew, of course, that she'd just unbuckled his belt, but this seemed more like a dream than reality. Liv would never...

"Are you sure no one is around?" He could see a dim corridor through the opening in the door, but he couldn't believe he'd asked.

She laughed softly and unzipped him, pushing

down his trousers. He needed to take them all the way off before he tripped, but he was mesmerized when she flipped off her shoes and slowly rolled her panty hose down to her ankles and stepped out of them. He was having a hard time catching his breath.

"This isn't like you." His voice sounded far away in his own ears.

"You taught me how to loosen up. It's what you want, isn't it?"

Her panties were red, a little scrap of nylon that she hung beside her panty hose on a bar that ran around the walls of the elevator. She was always neat. That hadn't changed, but the Olivia Kearns he knew certainly had.

She loosened his tie and unbuttoned his shirt so it hung open under his jacket. He felt silly standing in white briefs and dark socks with one shoe off, but he was burning to know what she'd do next. He'd never expected to see the day when Liv would seduce him in a public elevator.

"Are you sure?" he murmured when she cradled her chin against his chest and delicately flicked her tongue over one of his nipples.

"Oh, yeah," she whispered.

He forgot about the why and wondered about the

how as she ran her fingernails down his ribs and under the elastic of his briefs.

He had a few seconds to think while she hung his necktie beside her panties and hose. What was that bar? Had the designers expected people to need a handhold on an elevator ride? Or maybe it was there in case an emergency required the occupants to climb up to the paneled opening in the roof.

He was trying to bring himself down by thinking of prosaic things. He was ready to come and didn't want to be a minuteman with Liv. She knelt, pulled down his briefs and moistened the tip of his penis with her tongue.

"Not yet, baby." He lifted her up and kissed her eyelids and the end of her nose.

"I was just going to—"

He cut her off by covering her mouth with his. He felt her quiver and held her even closer, lifting her skirt so there was nothing separating their flesh.

He'd forgotten he could feel this way, not just aroused but deliriously happy. Liv was doing the wildest thing possible, something he'd never expect her to do.

But he had had high hopes for the evening. Before meeting her for the party, he'd made a purchase. He bent and fumbled in his trousers pocket, finding the strip of foil packets.

"Did you expect to need those at the party?" Her voice sounded sultry.

"You know I've always been a optimist."

She took the packet from him, carefully opened it and put the wrapper in her little purse sitting in a corner of the elevator. He grinned because Liv was Liv, always tidy, but she'd never been more desirable, more beautiful or more eager. She got him ready with far less fumbling than he could've managed, locked her hands behind his neck and pulled his head down to hers.

She kissed him. She tongued him. She tipped him over the edge. He lifted and penetrated her in a move so fluid and smooth they could've been practicing for ages. Then his mind went blank in the vise of her legs. She helped as she never had before, riding him with wild gyrations. He wanted to go on for hours, but when she climaxed with convulsion after convulsion, he came, too.

He was stunned. Great sex, yes, but also a connection that went beyond it. He'd felt part of her, totally in sync. He didn't want to pull away because it meant separation.

She dropped her legs and stood on the tops of his feet.

"You're good, Matheson."

He felt inordinately proud of himself even though

his more rational, cynical self told him it had been her show. She'd initiated it. He'd been putty in her hands, and he'd loved every second of it.

She wiggled away and slipped into her panties, dressing so gracefully in the confined space that she made it seem like a ballet. She was fully clothed before he could bring himself to look away and get his pants on.

He wanted to hold her and kiss her, but the elevator door slid shut and the cage moved downward.

"Do we have to go back to the party?" Was that hoarse rasp really his voice?

"Only to get our coats." She grinned at him with lush pink lips then winked.

He'd never seen her wink. What other surprises did she have for him? He cared more about Liv than he wanted to admit to himself. How would he feel if they split again? He hated the idea, but even more he loathed the idea that he might be responsible for hurting her again.

13

LIV WOKE UP the morning after the party with a smile on her face. Nick was curled up beside her under the covers. She snuggled against his backside and decided cuddling was almost as satisfying as sex. She rubbed her toes against the soft hair on his calves and leaned close to tickle his ear with her breath.

"It's nearly noon," she said softly. She loved Billy Lawrence for insisting no one go near the office on Christmas Eve.

"Good, but I'm not a morning person." He yanked the covers over his head and pretended to go back to sleep.

"I guess you deserve your rest."

He moved so quickly she shrieked, then claimed a morning kiss that left her breathless.

"Mind if I use your shower?" he asked.

"I'm willing to share."

"The bad news is I have to go into the office."

"What's the good news?"

Her question was more than casual. She needed to hear that their lovemaking meant as much to him as it did to her. She was desperate to hear how he felt about her now.

"The good news is that you're a dynamite woman." He kissed her forehead and sat up, letting the covers fall to his waist. "I'm glad I'm the one you got spontaneous with."

As if any man had ever mattered to her the way he did, Liv thought, her happy mood dissolving. What had she started? Was she setting herself up for more pain? She was very much afraid she was, but she didn't have the willpower to push Nick out of her life.

She watched him get out of bed and walk naked across the room to the adjoining bathroom. She felt unsatisfied in a way she couldn't pin down.

She ached at the sight of him. He was tall but not gangly, muscular without the bulkiness of a guy who pumped iron and graceful without trying to be. And darned if he didn't have the cutest butt imaginable, smooth with round squeezable cheeks.

She didn't want to be in love with him, but she didn't want to give him up either. He wanted spontaneity. She'd give him spontaneity. He was so much better off with her than without her, but he had a lone-wolf mentality.

He'd made it crystal clear when they were together before that he might never be ready for commitment. He'd blamed his career aspirations. She knew better, but would he ever realize how wrong he was? He'd told her about his father's dismal record with faithfulness and his own fears of being the same way.

She wasn't worried about other women in his life, as she had been when they were younger. Now she knew it was his determination to go it alone that really stood between them. Not once in their passionate, mind-boggling sexual encounters had he slipped up and said he loved her.

"What are you doing for Christmas?" he asked when he came out of the shower with one of her peach bath towels wrapped around his middle.

"Nothing."

"Where are your parents?"

"Mom's in Wisconsin with Amy and her fiancé. Dad's in Florida with his parents."

"I'm really sorry about everything that's been happening with your family," he said sympathetically. "I know what you're going through. I made myself miserable over my parents' divorce," he confessed. "You were great to put up with me. But it's history. They both seem happy, and I'm happy for them. So what are you doing over the holidays?"

"I have a lot of work I can do at home."

"You can't spend Christmas working. Even the

Post gives people the day off, except for a skeleton staff that doesn't include me."

She was sitting in bed with the covers bunched under her chin.

"We'll spend Christmas together," he said.

"Aren't you going to your dad's or something?"

"No, he's going to his wife's folks."

She worried her plan had failed. Far from getting Nick out of her system by having wild, uninhibited sex, she was starting to care far too much. Would he ever let down his emotional guard? Was she wasting her love on a man who was incapable of accepting it?

"How about it?" Nick was putting on the wrinkled dress shirt he'd thrown on the floor last night.

"I don't think so."

"Not a good answer. You can't spend Christmas alone. Let me rephrase the question. Your place or mine?"

"Really, Nick, I have plenty of work to keep me occupied, and I'll have to make a lot of Christmas phone calls."

"Okay, my place it is. I'll fix dinner. Do your work, make your calls and come as soon as you can. Or I'll come and get you."

"No, don't do that." If she did go, she wanted to be able to arrive and leave on her own.

He talked as though they would soon be intimate again. Being with Nick made her feel alive and wanted, but was it enough? She was trying, but could she do this without knowing how he felt and what he wanted?

Nick had a great gift with words, but he didn't say the ones that would allow them to understand each other better.

He dressed hurriedly, leaving his tie in a loose knot and bending to plant a hasty kiss on the top of her bed-mussed hair.

"See you tomorrow. If you're not at my place by five o'clock, I'll come here."

Had she agreed to spend Christmas with him? She didn't think so. Was she going to go? She knew she didn't have the willpower to resist seeing Nick one more time, then one more time again. She imagined herself at her mother's age still vowing to put Nick out of her life as soon as she saw him one more time.

The day of Christmas Eve seemed very long. Nick called as she was getting ready for bed. She loved the timbre of his voice on the phone. She loved that he'd called to suggest the easiest way to drive from her place to his. She felt a renewed shiver of desire when he told her how much he'd enjoyed being with her, but when he hung up, she was more depressed than ever.

Christmas Day she made her calls early. Mom, Dad, her Florida grandparents and her other grandparents did all they could to assure her they were fine except for missing her. Amy spoke with a stilted gaiety that told Liv other people were in the room with her sister.

Liv could've gone to Nick's at one o'clock for all the work she'd accomplished. Her brain was numb, and she couldn't seem to come up with a single fresh idea to present to the sports-bar owners.

The day was sunny and bright with a light layer of fresh snow that sparkled like diamonds, but by five o'clock it would start to get dark. She used that as an excuse to leave for Nick's earlier than she'd intended.

Once, she'd challenged Nick, wanting a commitment he refused to give. If she did that now, would he leave her again? Did she want to be with him without knowing where she stood? For now, she did, but she had deep reservations about the future.

She dressed in faded jeans and an oversize ski sweater. Instead of letting a lock of hair sweep forward on the side of her face the way her beautician had cut it, she tucked it severely behind her ears and anchored both sides with small hair clips.

Then she found a bottle of wine to contribute to

the occasion, and she was off, wanting to see Nick but not at all sure it was a good thing for her.

Even without much traffic, it took nearly half an hour to get to Nick's apartment complex in Ira Heights. She couldn't help but smile at the haphazard design of the apartments that incorporated every building material available in the Great Lakes area. She found Nick's number easily enough and parked in a space right across from his door. Residents seemed to have deserted the complex in droves, if the lack of window lights and the abundance of parking spaces were any indication.

NICK WAS RELIEVED when Liv got to his place. He hadn't been sure she'd show, so he sagged with relief when she got out of her car and came toward his door.

"Merry Christmas," he said from the doorway, wanting to give her a big bear hug but hesitant about their status. They were lovers again, but were they friends? All he knew for sure was that he wanted to be with her.

"Merry Christmas." She stepped inside and handed him a bottle of wine. "It's getting colder outside."

Weather was a safe topic. He contributed a couple of pithy comments relative to snow and temperature, but she was too busy taking off her coat and boots to answer. So far she'd looked above and beyond him, not making eye contact.

"You've decorated for Christmas," she said, sounding genuinely touched.

"I gave it a shot."

"More than that. You have a real tree."

She stepped forward to admire the scraggly little leftover evergreen he'd picked up on the way home yesterday. It was such a poor specimen that he'd had the seller saw off the bottom half before he agreed to buy it, but it seemed important to make the gesture for Liv's sake. It was probably the first time she hadn't spent Christmas at her parents' home.

"Where did you get the decorations?" She touched a mouse with a baseball bat hung on a scrawny branch.

"I had them as a kid. Mom made me take a box of trim and lights when she moved to Florida. This is the first time I've had them out."

"Something smells good," Liv said. "I never knew you to cook."

"I'm just heating up a deli chicken. We're having a seven-course dinner, all in plastic containers."

"Sounds great. I skipped lunch."

"You made all your calls? How is everyone?"

"Fine."

"Get all your work done?"

"I wasn't very creative today."

"Happens."

They'd always had things to talk about in the past, but right now Nick couldn't come up with a single topic. Maybe hot sex was detrimental to his brain. He wanted to research that in a hands-on way, but Liv seemed to have a force field protecting her.

"Well, why don't you open your present," he said, bending to retrieve it.

"I didn't bring one for you," she said.

"The wine counts. Open the package."

They sat down on his leather couch with a yard of space between them, and he passed the holiday-wrapped gift down its length to her.

"Very festive," she said, fingering a red ribbon. "But you shouldn't have…"

"I wanted to. Open it."

She was opening it with maddening slowness. As she took off the lid, her face told him all he needed to know.

"Nick! It's lovely!" She held the cameo brooch in the palm of her hand and looked ready to cry.

"We lost my great-grandmother a few years ago. Mom gave me a few pieces of her jewelry because there was more than she'd ever wear."

"This is a family heirloom. I can't take it." She

gazed down at the carved-shell face of a woman, white on black and set in gold. "It's so beautiful!"

She came into his arms and kissed his lips, giving him a chance for the bear hug he'd wanted more with each passing second. For now, holding her was enough.

"This was so thoughtful of you," she said.

"I'm glad you like it. I'll pour your wine, then we can eat."

"Great. I'm absolutely starving. What do you have besides chicken?"

"The usual Christmas fare. Macaroni and potato salads, cranberry gelatin, stuff like that."

They ate at the kitchen table after he carved up the roasted chicken. He loved seeing Liv eat, but he wasn't particularly hungry himself, at least not for anything that came in a deli container.

For the first time in his checkered history with women, he felt awkward and unsure. He wanted to do everything they'd done after the office party, but even more, he wanted her to wake up in his bed. Unfortunately the evening didn't seem to be going that way. He felt oddly unsure of himself, something that had never happened before with Liv.

"I should go home now," she said after dinner.

"I wish you wouldn't." He took her hand in his and kissed her knuckles.

"Tomorrow is another day," she said.

"Don't go yet."

"It's better if I do. Thank you for the brooch. It's a lovely gift."

"Stay a while longer."

"If I stay with you tonight, what about tomorrow and the next day and the next?"

"Can't you take life one day at a time?"

"I'm trying to change, Nick, but it's hard."

"We know each other well enough to be honest, Liv. I very much want to be with you. Isn't that enough for now?"

"I thought it might be, but I want a relationship that lasts. You're the one not being honest. How do you really feel about me?" Her face was flushed, and her eyes had never looked brighter.

He couldn't fit into Liv's paint-by-number view of life any more than she could permanently morph into the free-spirited, live-for-the-minute sex partner she'd briefly been in the elevator.

But he wasn't ready to give up. She'd triggered something in him that he'd thought was long gone, the same feeling he'd had when they were first together.

"I think an awful lot of you."

"But?"

"I'm not sure I'll ever be ready to change the way

you want. My father never has, and my mother paid the price. I don't want that to happen between us."

"So you're afraid of taking a chance."

"No, I'm afraid of letting you down again," he said. "I want to be with you, but I don't want us to delude ourselves. It might not work for long, but that isn't a reason to deny ourselves the pleasure of being together."

"I understand," she said.

She started putting on her boots. He wanted to stop her from leaving more than he'd ever wanted anything, but he didn't know how to be the man she wanted.

"Maybe you're right." It was the hardest thing he'd ever said. "Maybe you should go."

"I am going." She had her coat on when she remembered the brooch she'd pinned to her sweater. "I can't keep this, Nick."

"I gave it to you. It's yours." He couldn't believe how much it hurt to see her fumbling to unpin the jewelry.

"No, I can't. It means too much to me."

"That doesn't make sense. If you like it—"

"It's not about liking. I love it! But it represents family and continuity and all the things that mean so much to me and nothing to you." She handed the brooch to him, and he felt as if he'd been slapped in the face.

She turned to go. Every fiber in his body wanted to stop her, but he couldn't bring himself to say the words that would keep her there.

14

LIV SPENT New Year's Eve with a messy head cold, her eyes watery and her nose flaming red. She told herself it was the season to be sick and had nothing to do with being depressed.

Dana had been adamant about taking her to a New Year's Eve party, practically guaranteeing she'd meet some divine male who would sweep her off her feet. Liv declined on the grounds that a runny nose was not date bait. Dana knew a little about Nick, but Liv couldn't tell anyone, not even her best friend, how devastated she felt. It wasn't pride that kept her from confiding in Dana. She just couldn't handle sympathy. Dana would cluck over her like a mother hen. Liv had to get over him in her own way, quietly and alone.

Nick had called a couple of days after Christmas. He was on his way out of town on an assignment. The sports world didn't take a break over the holidays. Their conversation had been short and impersonal. She didn't know why he'd bothered to call at all.

New Year's Day was bleak and gray, hardly a good omen for the start of a new year. Just when Liv thought her life couldn't get worse, Amy came to see her.

"Christmas was horrible," her sister said as soon as they were seated at the kitchen table with cups of hot tea. "I've never been so stressed."

"Was it a problem having Mom there?" Liv sniffed and reached for another tissue.

"No, not really. You could tell her heart wasn't in it, but she didn't do anything to spoil Christmas for the rest of us."

"Tell me why you're upset," she said.

"Sean and I had a terrible fight," Amy said miserably. "He thinks I'm too stressed out to be around. He said I always make a big deal out of nothing. And he meant our wedding. He slept at a friend's last night. Right now I'm not even sure we love each other enough to get married. What should I do?"

Liv took a deep breath. Her head ached, and she didn't know what to say to her sister. How could she mastermind someone else's love life when her own was a shambles?

Did she believe in the power of love anymore? She'd loved Nick with her whole heart, and he probably had loved her a little in his own way, but that was little consolation.

"You should talk it over with him as soon as possible," Liv told her sister.

"You're right," Amy said after a thoughtful silence. "I guess Sean and I have to talk before our wedding plans go any further."

Amy hugged her and left, and Liv nursed her cold through the weekend. At least she did come up with a few strong ideas about how to get the sports-bar account. The bars should be presented as feel-good places where people could share their interest in sports. She hadn't been doing her best work because she'd lacked enthusiasm. Once she started thinking of the bars as more than jock hangouts, she could see all kinds of potential for a public relations agenda.

By the time she went to work on Monday, her cold was gone and her ideas had crystallized. She didn't need Nick Matheson to have a successful life, which was a darn good thing because she hadn't heard from him in over a week. She had one week to polish her presentation, and it was going to be great.

She had to do the background research herself, but she didn't miss Brandi Jo's help. In fact, it felt wonderful to have the office all to herself again. She didn't have to watch every word she said. She didn't need to guard her computer screen against the prying eyes of an intern intent on snagging her job.

For the first time in quite a while, she was enthusiastic about work. Ideas flowed, and when thoughts of Nick intruded, she forced them out of her mind.

When the phone rang shortly after eleven, she answered reluctantly, not welcoming interruptions. She'd almost forgotten about Matilda Merris, but the elderly woman was true to her word. She'd called to give Liv her decision.

"I'll talk to the young man from the *Post* on the telephone," she said, "but I won't promise anything until he answers my questions. Could you give me his number, please?"

"That's wonderful, Miss Merris. I hope the two of you can come up with a way to include your father's memorabilia in the new museum."

She gave Matilda Merris Nick's work and home numbers, then ended the conversation, happy to cross her off her list of things to do.

By Wednesday morning she knew Nick wasn't going to call. She might never hear from him again, and the pain increased with each passing day. She wasn't sleeping well, and her town house seemed dreary and empty for the first time since she'd moved there. Maybe she'd been kidding herself all along. She'd had the crazy idea that she could change for him, that she could be wild and uninhibited. She'd succeeded in attracting his attention again, but they were no closer to having a real relationship than they'd ever been.

Boz barged into her office early Wednesday morning looking unusually red-faced and flustered.

"The time for your sports-bar presentation has been changed. J. B. Davenport can't make it next Monday, so you have to make your pitch Thursday."

"This Thursday, as in tomorrow?"

"Is it a problem?"

Liv wondered how much he had riding on her bid for a new client.

"No, I'm nearly ready." She watched him sag with relief and guessed he needed a career boost himself now that he had to work for a new-generation Lawrence.

"Great! If there's anything you need, anything at all, let me know, and I'll make it top priority."

"When and where?"

"You're meeting J. B. Davenport in suite 752 at the Pentland Hotel. Be there at twelve sharp. Here's a company credit card so you can sign for lunch."

By Thursday morning Liv should've been a nervous wreck, but she felt calm about meeting a potential client. She was glad to have a distraction that would get Nick out of her mind. She'd get the account or she wouldn't, but either way she had to get on with her life. She wasn't going to go through life like a zombie on the fast track to nowhere.

She laid out her leather skirt, but couldn't decide what to wear on top. When it came time to put on the sexy outfit, she balked. Her presentation would be great. She wasn't going to wear skimpy clothes to titillate a stranger she was meeting in a hotel suite. If he was dumb enough to turn down what William Lawrence Associates could do for the sports-bar chain, it was his loss.

She left the skirt on the unmade bed and put on a sleekly styled brown pantsuit with a white shirt. It was her best business suit, and she looked attractive and professional.

When she got to work, people seemed to tiptoe around her. They weren't exactly unfriendly. *Guarded* was a better word, as though everyone knew she was going into battle and didn't want to be associated too closely with failure. Dana was the only one who wished her good luck with an encouraging hug.

The phone was ringing when she walked into her office. She hoped it didn't mean another time change for her big presentation.

"Liv, how are you?" Nick didn't need to identify himself. His voice rippled through her, making her shiver.

"Fine." Her tongue felt two inches thick.

"Thanks for giving Matilda my number. There's one small problem though. She wants to see you too."

"Me? I have nothing to do with your story."

"I guess she liked talking to you. Anyway she'll trust me more if you're with me," he said. "I'm supposed to see her this afternoon. Can you come with me?"

"I have my big presentation at noon. I have no idea how long it will take."

"Too bad. I would've liked you along for the ride. The weather is supposed to get bad later this evening, so I made a reservation at the Blossom Motel in Saint Joe."

"You could change your appointment if the roads are going to be bad," she said. Or if he didn't want to go without her.

"No, today is Marty's birthday. His daughter thinks it's the right day to finally open up about what really caused the scandal."

"Sorry I can't go." She would like to be with him, but it probably wouldn't solve the stalemate in their relationship. She'd become resigned to the fact that there was no hope for a future with him.

"Goodbye, Nick."

Things might never work out with Nick, but one

part of her had changed: her attitude. She went to the hotel suite determined to give the best presentation in the history of the agency. Talking to Nick had only boosted her self-confidence. Either the client would like her ideas or he was an idiot. She went up on the fast, silent elevator determined to succeed.

She only had to knock once on the door of the suite. A middle-aged woman with salt-and-pepper hair, sharp features and wire-rimmed glasses and wearing a black suit opened the door.

"You must be from William Lawrence Associates," she said in a businesslike voice. "I'm J. B. Davenport."

"Yes, I'm Olivia Kearns," she said, offering her hand for a firm shake.

In spite of her mild shock that J. B. Davenport was a woman, Liv had the presence of mind not to show it.

"I ordered lean roast-beef sandwiches and spinach salad," the tall, slender woman said. "They brought them five minutes early. I'm pleased you know how to arrive right on the minute."

"I've been accused of being a control freak, but I like being on schedule." Liv surprised herself by being so up front, but J.B.'s smile was warm.

"Good. My partners think I'm one too, but they're too busy picking out TVs for the bars and finding memorabilia to hang on the walls to worry about dollars and cents." She led the way to a small table set with a white linen cloth and covered dishes.

Liv didn't have an answer to that. She put down her attaché case and purse and dropped her coat on a chair. She had a brief moment of discomfort when J.B. looked her over from hair neatly tucked behind her ears to chunky-heeled tan boots.

"What a relief to meet a woman who knows how to dress for business," J.B. said.

Liv allowed herself one small self-satisfied smile, then settled down across from J.B. at the little table. This was going to be the presentation of a lifetime.

She got back to the office three hours later, still awed by J. B. Davenport's shrewdness and decisiveness. She'd punched holes in every phase of the presentation, and Liv had defended it like a mother tiger. Miracle of miracles, she'd walked out of the suite with a deal ready for the lawyers to finalize.

Boz gave her a hearty handshake, a sure indication of her enhanced status. Billy even came out of his office to congratulate her, an almost unprecedented event. The office staff theorized that he spent most of the day practicing his golf putting.

Unfortunately her euphoria faded fast, not that she wasn't proud of what she'd done. She'd proven herself without compromising her standards. A woman could be herself and still succeed.

But feeling as she did about Nick, it was a hollow victory. The emptiness returned, and her life seemed bleak. Maybe it didn't matter whether they were together for days or years. Maybe she was a fool not to snatch every second of happiness that she could.

Her phone rang when she was alone in her office again. She desperately hoped it was Nick.

It was Amy. She sounded breathless and agitated, so Liv slumped down on her chair expecting the worst.

"I did what you said!" Amy said. "I went to Sean's office first thing this morning, then waited for him to get to work. I knew he'd be stunned, because I'm not a morning person."

Liv was sure she'd never suggested anything remotely like that plan, but Amy did have her full attention.

"When he got there, I was cool, calm and collected."

"Good for you."

"He locked the door, and we had a long talk. It was incredible! He was worried about the same things I was. We had a big collective case of pre-wedding anxiety. We *were* meant to be together, Liv.

I know it now! We couldn't be happier or more in love. Thank you for helping me."

"Amy, I'm really happy for you, but it was all your doing. You're the spontaneous one. You knew just what to do."

"I did, didn't I?" Amy said happily. "I was an hour late to work, but they didn't even dock me. Business will be slack until Valentine's Day, but that will give me more time for Sean. I hope things work out this well for you and Nick."

"That's not likely. I don't even know whether I should see him again. He's not into commitment. Never was and most likely never will be."

"Too bad. I like him. So do you, if you're honest with yourself. You could play it by ear, you know, not rush things. It might turn out better than you think."

"Or worse."

"I can't imagine anything worse than not seeing Sean anymore."

Liv realized with a start that she felt the same way. It would be awful if she never saw Nick again. The question was, what could she do about it?

"When you're right, you're dead right," Liv told her sister.

"I am? Well, happy to give you a big sister's

words of wisdom. Call me sometime soon. Bye now."

Liv hadn't helped Amy. Her sister had helped herself by listening to her heart. Maybe it was time Liv paid attention to hers.

15

NICK LOCATED Matilda Merris's house, hopeful that this time he wouldn't have to stand outside looking pathetic. Marty's daughter had sounded eager to meet Liv, but she hadn't exactly refused to see him alone.

The street was narrow, and the small houses were close together with little lawns in front. Her graystone two-story house was larger than the bungalows tucked on either side, but like all the homes nearby, it looked old and weathered.

Looks were deceiving though. This was probably some of the most coveted property in the small lakeside town of Saint Joseph because it was only a block or so from the sandy beach of Lake Michigan. Nick had to give the residents credit for hanging on to their homes. He liked the character of the street a whole lot better than a monotonous block of condos.

He wished Liv was with him, and it had nothing to do with Merris. Lately he'd been having long conversations with her in his head. He was trying to get a handle on how he felt, but more and more he just wanted to be with her.

He had a game plan for interviewing Matilda, but he didn't have his usual intensity. He loved going after hard stories and getting difficult people to talk, but today he felt listless. He'd score points big-time with his editor if he came through on this, but he was having trouble concentrating on anything but Liv.

He rang the doorbell. The icy breeze blowing off the lake cut through his jacket. The inner door opened, and Nick found himself looking through a glass storm door at an older but certainly not an elderly woman. Matilda Merris was lean and wiry, nearly as tall as he was, if her shoulders weren't stooped with age. She had the lined, leathery face of a sun lover, her long gray hair pulled back in a ponytail and sharp blue eyes.

She cracked the storm door and said, "Mr. Matheson from the *Chicago Post*, I assume."

"Yes, ma'am." She was the kind of woman who commanded the respectful use of "ma'am."

"The young lady didn't come with you?"

"I'm sorry. She couldn't get away from work."

"Well, come in," Matilda said, pushing the door open.

He stomped snow on her woven doormat and

stood on the flagstone entryway prepared to take off his boots.

"Never mind," she said, leading the way to a central staircase covered in worn beige carpeting.

She didn't give him much chance to look around, but the small rooms on either side looked more like art galleries than rooms for living. The walls of the hallway and stairs were crowded with mosaics made of everything from eggshells to chunks of broken plates. Driftwood sculptures sat on the floor along with old and broken furniture parts assembled to suggest monsters.

Matilda was wearing jeans and a blue oxford shirt that hugged her lean thighs as she led him up the stairs. The second floor consisted of a large workshop with a skylight in the ceiling and sliding glass doors leading off to a wooden deck. He caught a glimpse of the dark wintry surface of Lake Michigan before she told him to take his coat off and toss it anywhere.

What had made him think he was going to interview a feeble old lady? She looked like the athlete's daughter she was.

She had coffee brewing in a pot on one of the workbenches lining the room. A plastic plate of graham crackers and some paper napkins were sitting on an old Formica-and-chrome kitchen table.

"Now," she said, pouring strong black coffee for

both of them without asking, "what about my father?"

Nick gave her the whole spiel about the museum directors refusing to accept his editor's collection of Marty Merris memorabilia. He had a feeling no one conned this woman, and he didn't try.

"That's pretty much what your girlfriend told me," she said thoughtfully.

Nick didn't correct her about Liv. Was she his girlfriend? No, she was more than that. He'd had girlfriends since eighth grade, but Liv was so special he was scared to define their relationship with such a bland term. He didn't want to think of life without her, but what if he committed himself and failed? What if their feelings changed the way his parents' had?

He realized Matilda was looking at him oddly, waiting for him to say something. He'd lost the thread of their conversation, the first time that had ever happened during an interview.

"You want to know why my father did it, don't you?"

He nodded. He wasn't going to pressure her, not even if it meant going back to his editor empty-handed, but he was hoping to hear the whole truth behind the scandal.

He let Matilda tell the story her own way without interruption. She talked a long time, as though she'd bottled up her father's tragic story for so long it was a relief to let the words flow.

"The press condemned my father. They weren't interested in the truth," she said sadly. "He refused to be interviewed ever again, even when he was old. After he died, I vowed never to let some vulture trample on his memory. Now that I'm old myself, maybe it's time to vindicate him."

Nick only vaguely noticed the early darkness of winter that cast gloom over the studio. Matilda told him a story of mobsters who threatened Marty's family if he didn't agree to throw the game.

"It was all about gambling," Matilda said, "but my father never doubted they'd kill my mother and me."

"He took the bribe?" Nick felt he had to ask, but he couldn't help hoping Marty Merris was worthy of his daughter's devotion.

She was quiet for so long, he didn't think she'd answer.

"He did," she said at last. "You want proof, of course. Wait here."

She flicked on a light over the stairs and went down, disappearing for so long Nick was afraid something had happened to her. He waited impatiently until she came back.

"Here." She put a battered tin pail that had originally held peanut butter in front of him. "Open it."

The cover was rusty, and he struggled to get it off. A bundle wrapped in yellowed newsprint was inside. He took it out and slowly unwrapped it, the old newspaper flaking off at his touch. It was money, lots of old bills secured by a rubber band that had rotted into hard, dark fragments.

"Is this the bribe?" he asked.

"Yes, my father never spent a penny of it, not even when he couldn't get any job except picking fruit in season."

Nick realized what a bad time this was to be a reporter without a photographer. Matilda had been so reluctant to see him that he hadn't wanted to put her off by arriving with one in tow.

"I'll need pictures of this," he said.

"Yes, I have a camera," Matilda said matter-of-factly.

He started to explain that it would have to be a professional photo, but she cut him off.

"I'm a professional photographer among other things," she said wryly. "When you're on your own, you pick up a lot of skills. My Lake Michigan wildlife photos paid for this house. I'll take your pictures."

She shot a whole roll, even letting him take a few of her with the money. He left Matilda Merris with the best story of his career, a roll of film to back it up and the feeling he'd made a new friend.

For once he wasn't in a rush to get back to his computer to write up what he'd learned. Marty's story had been on hold for nearly seventy years. He wanted to give it his very best efforts.

The dark drive home wasn't appealing, so he decided to head for the Blossom Motel in Saint Joe, glad that he'd had the foresight to make a reservation.

LIV LEFT HER OFFICE early, took a train to the Roselle station and got her car. Without bothering to go home first, she headed south, back into the congestion of late-afternoon Chicago traffic. She figured it would take a couple of hours to drive around the tip of the lake to Michigan, but she was too optimistic. The multitude of tollbooths were frustrating bottlenecks, and by the time traffic thinned, she had serious doubts about what she was doing.

She only stopped once for gas and a fast-food burger, but it was still nearly eight o'clock when she exited the interstate and made her way into Saint Joseph. She didn't have a clue where the Blossom Motel was, and she was a little worried that Nick might have gone back to Chicago instead of checking in for the night.

The town wasn't that big, but rather than drive around in the snow that was coming down harder and harder, she stopped at a service station with an outdoor phone. She shivered in the icy lake-effect wind and found a battered phone directory hanging on a chain. The ad in the directory showed a map with the location of the motel, but she got even colder standing there memorizing it.

A semi pulled into the service station and spotlighted Liv in its high beams. She felt like a B-movie prison escapee caught by a guard's searchlight. Did this mean she felt guilty about trying to track down the man she loved? What was the worst that could happen? If Nick sent her away, it would confirm that he didn't love her. No matter how much it hurt, at least when her hope died, she could get on with the rest of her life.

Big fluffy snowflakes landed on her windshield as she drove to the Blossom Motel. Liv easily found a parking spot in the half-empty lot where snow was rapidly accumulating.

A sleepy-eyed desk clerk gave her Nick's room number without any hesitation, something that would never have happened in Chicago. One of two small elevator cages was waiting at the lobby level, and she rode up to the second floor trying not to remember how fantastic it had been to make love with Nick in an elevator.

Room 216 seemed a long way from where she got off, considering the low number, or maybe it only seemed that way because she was nervous about seeing him. Her anxiety peaked when he didn't come to the door for several long moments after she knocked. Why was she here? How did she expect him to react? How could she change anything by showing up at his motel?

Then he was framed in the open doorway, and her mind went blank.

"Liv."

Nick looked astonished. He stared at her with azure-blue eyes, and his lips parted as though he wanted to say something but couldn't get it out.

Her heart contracted, and she was afraid she was going to lose this beautiful man forever. She could feel the tension between them enveloping like her like a dense fog. What should she say?

In the background the room was lit by a reading light on the desk and another between two double beds. Nick looked comfortable in the subdued light. The top snap on his khaki trousers was open, and his dark green shirt was unbuttoned. He was wearing heavy white crew socks with no shoes, and she was struck by his ability to look completely at home no matter where he was.

"I was in the neighborhood." She forced herself to flash a weak smile.

"Come in," he said softly.

"It's snowing pretty hard." The flakes captured in her hair were melting, and she brushed aside a trickle of water on her forehead before she stepped into the room.

The door clicked shut automatically behind her. Nick had backed up to let her enter, and the distance between them seemed far greater than a paltry couple of feet.

"How was your meeting with Matilda?" she asked.

"Fantastic." His lips scarcely moved when he answered. He was totally immobile, as though frozen stiff.

"You found something to vindicate Marty Merris?"

"Gangsters made him do it. Matilda still has the money they paid him. He never spent a penny. He took the bribe because the mob threatened to kill his family."

"Nick, that's wonderful! I mean, it's a tragic story, but his name will be cleared. They'll have to include him in the sports museum now."

"Hopefully. How did your meeting go?" he asked.

"It couldn't have gone better. I won the client over for William Lawrence Associates."

"Congratulations. But why are you here?" He sounded stunned.

"I don't like the way we left things between us."

She walked around him and dropped her purse

on the foot of the nearest bed, where the burgundy-and-blue bedspread hadn't been disturbed. Afraid of losing her nerve if she hesitated, she took off her coat and sat on the edge, looking up at him while she tried to find the words she needed.

"I don't either," he said, pulling up a desk chair so he could face her. "Liv, I'm sorry..."

"I didn't come for an apology."

"You deserve one, though. I've done a lot of thinking. We've been in a time warp, reliving the good and the bad that happened between us five years ago. We should've started over fresh. To your credit, you tried to change."

"And bombed." She smiled wryly. "I found out I want the same things I wanted then. I'm only spontaneous when I plan it out."

He laughed and leaned forward to take her hand. "You're a great planner—and more woman than I deserve. When I started facing the prospect of not having you in my life, I hated it. I want you to—"

"Don't say anything you'll regret, Nick, anything we'll both regret. I wouldn't want a commitment unless you were completely sure."

"You wouldn't get one. I was about to say, I want you to know that I love you. Without you I'm just a guy who writes sports stories. My byline is my identity. I didn't know I was incomplete until I realized how much you mean to me."

"I...I don't know what you're saying."

"I'm saying I want you in my life, not just today or tomorrow but way down the line, as long as you can put up with me."

"I probably won't change. I'll still be controlling and uptight and—"

"Sweet, considerate, intelligent—and don't forget sexy."

He took her hand between both of his, bringing her fingertips to his lips.

"This is the place where you tell me to get lost—or not." His voice was soft and beseeching.

"I choose 'or not.'" She felt light-headed, still a little afraid to believe they had a future together.

"Good choice." He stood and pulled her into his arms.

They stood, her face cradled against his chest, while he murmured things she'd been hoping to hear without the slightest expectation of doing so.

"I love you."

"I love you, too." She'd never said the words aloud to him. It was like relinquishing her innermost secret. She couldn't believe how warm and wonderful it felt.

"You never cease to amaze me," he whispered, gently touching her face with his lips. "You're the only person I know who can change and stay the same, only better."

"That doesn't make sense."

"I guess not, but being together does." They wrapped their arms around each other, hugging so tight she felt like part of him.

She expected him to kiss her again, to caress her, but instead he stood and looked down at her with hooded eyes, slowly shaking his head.

"What's wrong?"

"I can't believe I'm getting a second chance."

"Believe." She reached up and stroked his face, loving the short little bristles and the firmness of his cheeks. When their lips met, it was more than a kiss. It was a melding of two people who belonged together.

They undressed each other slowly like two people who had the rest of their lives to make love. She loved the taut skin of his chest and his slender waist.

Would the Nick she knew five years ago have been so gentle and restrained? He kissed her as though they had all the time in the world. Gradually he made her believe they did.

"Sweetheart." He scooped her into his arms and carried her to the bed, somehow managing to rip off the spread and blanket before he lowered her to the sheet. The most incredible sensation rippled down her spine as he caressed her neck and shoulders with his lips.

"Do you have any idea how dangerous it is to

show up at a man's door in the middle of the night?''
he teased as he lay beside her and pulled her into his
arms.

They slowly kissed, his breath warm on her face
and his hands gently stroking her. She held his head
between her hands, kissing his forehead, his cheeks
and ears until their lips came together for a long,
deep kiss.

He kissed her so hungrily she felt blessed, needing
and wanting nothing but him. She was only fully
alive when she was with Nick, and for the first time
ever she felt that they had all the time in the world to
consummate their love.

He tenderly kissed her breasts. He made sexy little
noises, and when he looked into her face, his features were softened by passion. She couldn't touch
him enough, stroking his back and buttocks as
though she could memorize the knobs of his spine
and the hard globes of muscle.

His lips moved lower, and she clutched his shoulders with her nails. Her breath caught as he readied
her with his tongue and fingers. She cried out when
he entered her and she spun out of control.

She always climaxed with Nick. He was a wizard
who could conjure up wild, undisciplined re-
sponses. She didn't hold back, not even when her
mind whirled and moans that seemed to come from

someone else drowned out Nick's passionate encouragement.

"Oh baby, oh, oh," he moaned.

Afterward he slid to his side, taking her with him so they stayed joined together.

"You were incredible." His voice sounded far away and drowsy as he pulled a cover over them and cradled her even closer against him.

She adored the fuzziness of his skin against hers. She loved the seductive scent of his body. She wanted to touch every part of him so she'd never forget the wonder of being with him.

Nick had always recuperated fast but never like tonight, never with so much urgency and intensity.

They made love, dozed and made love again. Always she woke up in his arms or pressed closely against him, and she knew this was where she wanted to be for the rest of her life. When she woke up in the murky grayness of morning, Nick was still sleeping. His lovemaking had made her too languid to get up and start dressing.

She was a new person because she didn't have to face empty days without him anymore. She'd come there hoping to maintain her link with Nick. She'd desperately wanted him to stay in her life on any terms, so much so she was almost afraid of her happiness.

"Good morning." He rolled closer and let his arm fall across her waist, locking her to him.

Most mornings her first waking act was to check the time. Today it didn't matter, because this was the beginning of the rest of her life.

BY THE TIME Nick got to his office it was midafternoon. He checked in with Mack, who was more than pleased with the news about Merris, then gave Kurt a short summary. He accepted a lot of congratulations, but nothing could make him any happier than he already was. He was walking on air because he knew what he really wanted in life, and that was Liv.

He'd always thought he was reasonably intelligent, but he'd been stupid when it came to Liv. He'd been too immature to realize how much she meant to him when he'd walked away from her five years ago. He wouldn't make the same mistake twice.

His day didn't really start until he met Liv in the lobby of her building after work.

"Italian?" he asked, taking her arm and tucking it into the crook of his arm.

"Anywhere as long as it's with you."

It was snowing again, driving flakes that whirled around them, but being with Liv was warmth enough for him. They walked slowly toward the Milano, indifferent to the wind and cold.

"I've been thinking all day," Liv said. "I can't help

loving you, but I don't want to trap you into a relationship that will make you hate me someday."

"I could never hate you!" He was upset that she could even think that. He stopped and pulled her into the circle of his arms, oblivious of people rushing past them to get out of the weather. She was so beautiful his eyes felt moist. "I've been a jerk," he began, feeling at a loss for words to say what he was feeling.

"Well, yes," she said in a teasing tone. "It's part of your charm."

He snorted, disgusted with himself because he didn't know how to say what he meant.

"I love you," he said.

She was absolutely still.

"I don't blame you if you're skeptical. I can hardly believe it myself. Nothing else in my life has ever been this wonderful. I love you, Liv. I really love you."

"How long have you felt that way?" Her voice was so low he had to strain to hear.

"I'm not sure. When we were together before, I was infatuated. I guess a lot of it was lust, although I'm not proud of that. But ever since we broke up—"

"You dumped me," she said. At least she didn't sound bitter.

"Since then there's always been something missing in my life. Now that I know what it was, I want us to be together."

He expected her to ask for particulars. Should they live together? Get engaged? Get married? Instead, she only smiled.

"It's what I want too. And I will try to be less controlling. I can change."

"You already have. Look at all the new confidence you have at work."

"I can change even more. For you."

"Don't even think about it," he said emphatically. "You're perfect for me."

Snow swirled and pedestrians skirted them. In their world everything was warm. Nick bent his head to kiss the woman he wanted to be his forever.

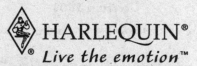

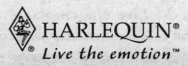

If you enjoyed what you just read,
then we've got an offer you can't resist!

Take 2 bestselling
love stories FREE!

Plus get a FREE surprise gift!

Clip this page and mail it to Harlequin Reader Service®

IN U.S.A.
3010 Walden Ave.
P.O. Box 1867
Buffalo, N.Y. 14240-1867

IN CANADA
P.O. Box 609
Fort Erie, Ontario
L2A 5X3

YES! Please send me 2 free Harlequin Temptation® novels and my free
surprise gift. After receiving them, if I don't wish to receive anymore, I can
return the shipping statement marked cancel. If I don't cancel, I will receive 4
brand-new novels each month, before they're available in stores. In the U.S.A.,
bill me at the bargain price of $3.57 plus 25¢ shipping and handling per book
and applicable sales tax, if any*. In Canada, bill me at the bargain price of $4.24
plus 25¢ shipping and handling per book and applicable taxes**. That's the
complete price and a savings of 10% off the cover prices—what a great deal!
I understand that accepting the 2 free books and gift places me under no
obligation ever to buy any books. I can always return a shipment and cancel at
any time. Even if I never buy another book from Harlequin, the 2 free books and
gift are mine to keep forever.

142 HDN DNT5
342 HDN DNT6

Name	(PLEASE PRINT)	
Address	Apt.#	
City	State/Prov.	Zip/Postal Code

* Terms and prices subject to change without notice. Sales tax applicable in N.Y.
** Canadian residents will be charged applicable provincial taxes and GST.
   All orders subject to approval. Offer limited to one per household and not valid to
   current Harlequin Temptation® subscribers.
   ® are registered trademarks of Harlequin Enterprises Limited.

TEMP02   ©1998 Harlequin Enterprises Limited

If you're a fan of sensual romance you *simply* must read…

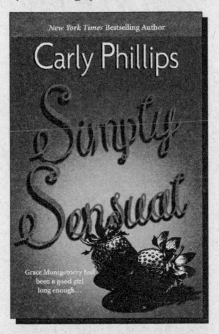

New York Times Bestselling Author

Carly Phillips

Simply Sensual

Grace Montgomery had been a good girl long enough…

The third sizzling title in Carly Phillips's *Simply* trilogy.

"4 STARS—Sizzle the winter blues away with a *Simply Sensual* tale…wonderful, alluring and fascinating!"
—*Romantic Times*

Available in January 2004.

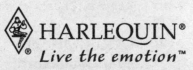

HARLEQUIN®
Live the emotion™

Visit us at www.eHarlequin.com

PHSSCP3

HARLEQUIN®

Temptation

THE WRONG BED

What happens when a girl finds herself in the
wrong bed...with the *right* guy?

Find out in:

#866 NAUGHTY BY NATURE by Jule McBride
February 2002

#870 SOMETHING WILD by Toni Blake
March 2002

#874 CARRIED AWAY by Donna Kauffman
April 2002

#878 HER PERFECT STRANGER by Jill Shalvis
May 2002

#882 BARELY MISTAKEN by Jennifer LaBrecque
June 2002

#886 TWO TO TANGLE by Leslie Kelly
July 2002

Midnight mix-ups have never been so much fun!

HARLEQUIN®
Makes any time special ®

Visit us at www.eHarlequin.com   HTNBN2